The Cowboy's Least Likely Bride

The Cowboy's Least Likely Bride

Family Matters of Cowboy Point

Megan Crane

TULE

The Cowboy's Least Likely Bride
Copyright© 2026 Megan Crane
Tule Publishing First Printing, February 2026

The Tule Publishing, Inc.

ALL RIGHTS RESERVED

First Publication by Tule Publishing 2026

Cover design by Lee Hyat Designs

No part of this book may be used or reproduced in any manner whatsoever without written permission except in the case of brief quotations embodied in critical articles and reviews.

This is a work of fiction. Names, characters, places, and incidents are products of the author's imagination or are used fictitiously. Any resemblance to actual events, locales, organizations, or persons, living or dead, is entirely coincidental.

AI was not used to create any part of this book and no part of this book may be used for generative training.

ISBN: 978-1-970840-34-6

Prologue

THE TWO WOMEN had their first in-person meeting on neutral ground. They picked a little coffee spot in Livingston, Montana—a good hour away from Marietta and even farther from Cowboy Point—where neither one of them lived.

They had both agreed that was best, for a variety of reasons.

After all, it wasn't every day that a woman went of her own volition to spend time with her late husband's other woman. The woman he'd been married to—however illegally wasn't really the point—for almost the whole time he'd also been married to her.

Jenny Lisle headed out that February morning, bright and early, easing her old Explorer down the frozen ruts in the dirt road that served as the main thoroughfare on Lisle Hill in Cowboy Point. The old hill on the west side of the tiny valley rose up from the General Store that had been here since the first miners came up from Marietta to look for a better life—not to mention some money and some land—all the way to the lighthouse on the high ridge at the top that her middle child, Dallas, had taken on and was renovating into a bed-and-breakfast.

A better use for the place than its time-honored position as a local eyesore, Jenny often thought, but never said out loud.

Folks around Cowboy Point got possessive about the past, eyesore or not. She'd learned that when she'd finally married her high school sweetheart and moved up here from Marietta, lo these many years ago now. Cowboy Point natives still considered her a newcomer.

Jenny didn't mind. It allowed her to get away with things. They could always blame it on her misbegotten youth ten miles down Copper Mountain with all those Marietta people who—everyone agreed—didn't really *understand* Cowboy Point.

This despite the fact that Cowboy Point was getting fancier and more accessible by the year, and was more and more a destination for the kind of Montanans who liked dude ranches better than rodeos. Or tourists who only wished they were Montanans, more like.

Jenny liked them all the same. They all spent their money in the quaint old General Store and took pictures out in front of the old sign that dated almost all the way back to the first iteration of the building, when it was little more than a shack with supplies to keep the miners fed.

At the bottom of Lisle Hill—a hill Jenny considered hers despite the fact she'd only married into the family, though it was true that she'd also kept the historic property in Lisle hands despite her former husband's best attempts to sell it so she figured it evened out—she paused as she looked at the

General Store, the diner that was attached to it, and the coffee cart in the parking lot that was now a year-round indulgence.

She wanted a cup of coffee. And she knew that if she went into the diner to get one, her eldest son, the regrettably over-responsible, overly serious, and sometimes downright grim Tennessee—and yes, she accepted that it was probably her fault that he was all of those things—would make it for her. He'd make it the way she liked it, light and sweet, even though she doubted he had ever polluted his own body with that much sugar or dairy. Tennessee was a man of many rules. He would make her coffee for her the way she liked it, but then he would want to know what she was doing and where she was going, and that was not a conversation she wished to have. Not yet.

Not until after this meeting of hers today.

The obvious solution was the coffee cart, but she couldn't bring herself to do it. This was because she had only gone to that cart and looked its owner straight in the face one time. Just once, and she'd known.

Because Helena Patrick, owner and primary barista of the coffee cart that had started out as a summer thing and was now considered a mainstay of the community, bore a striking resemblance to Jenny's youngest, Cat.

They could be sisters, she'd thought.

And given who her husband had been, Jenny had understood at once that it was very likely that they were.

So when the call came not long after Helena had appeared in Cowboy Point, Jenny hadn't been surprised. She'd known who her husband was, though she was ashamed to admit that she'd spent some years pretending she didn't. Jenny had been fully aware that charming, golden-boy Patrick Lisle was a cheater back in high school, so who was really to blame for the wreck of their marriage when she'd had that information and stayed with him anyway? Patrick had told her, repeatedly, that she had always known exactly what she was signing up for and it had always made her cry.

Probably because she'd known that he was right, she thought now.

But she'd been younger in those years, and she had lied to herself a whole lot more back then. Jenny was older now and she knew two things. One, that the lies a person told herself always, *always* came back to haunt her tenfold. And two, that she couldn't change a person who didn't want to be changed.

It was just too bad that she'd learned both of those critical things the hard way.

Still, it had felt like a fresh knife sunk deep into her sternum to discover who that voice on the other end of the line belonged to.

"My name is Peyton Patrick," the decidedly female voice had said, and Jenny had known who she was, who she had to be, immediately.

In some ways, she'd been waiting for this call since high school.

It was the way the other woman said her name. Even the hint of the South in her voice couldn't wash away the nerves. Or the hint of something more like a sadness that Jenny knew too well, because she felt it too.

"How can I help you?" Jenny had asked, maybe because she was trying to buy time. Or convince the other woman not to do the thing she had clearly called to do.

"I don't know that you *can* help me," the other woman had said, with a rueful laugh that had seemed to resonate deep inside Jenny whether she liked it or not. "I don't know how to say this nicely, I'm afraid, and I'm sorry for that. But I'm pretty sure that we were both married to the same man. At the same time."

Jenny didn't remember much about that initial conversation.

She'd been too shocked, and then furious with herself for the shock. Because again, she'd known Patrick. It had just never occurred to her that instead of having a woman in every port of call, he'd instead dragged a single, specific woman around with him out there, called her his wife, and had made a family with her. All the while coming home to Cowboy Point and his first family, where he'd either charmed them all silly or had pretended Jenny was the one responsible for those odd shadows and dark spaces in their marriage.

Maybe it was a good thing that she'd been too shocked to react much to Peyton that first time. It meant she had time to have her emotions later. In private. That was the only place she let herself really let go and cry these days.

But they'd agreed to speak again. And the second time, she had been slightly more prepared.

"Helena," she'd said when the other woman called at the

appointed time. She hadn't even bothered to say hello. "Is Helena your daughter?"

Peyton had let out a breath. "She surely is. And she's as hardheaded as they come. Once she found out about Cowboy Point, and the whole Lisle family there, well. Nothing could have kept her away."

The coffee cart hadn't been around that long, Jenny had thought. That meant Helena had been observing her half-family for a while.

Patrick had called himself *Lyle Patrick* for his second family. He hadn't even had the creativity to pick different names. He was *Patrick Lisle* at home in Cowboy Point, and had clearly made it so he could answer to the name in either direction.

Jenny really did have to admire the efficiency of it all.

When it didn't make her feel sick, that was.

"Helena has been talking so much about Cowboy Point that she's convinced her brothers to come check the place out," Peyton had told her. "And I felt I needed to reach out to you, because I don't think it's necessarily fair for us all to descend upon you without you having any idea that it's happening. Or even that we existed in the first place."

"I knew," Jenny admitted. She'd been sitting in her house then, curled up on the couch, in the historic Victorian that some or other Lisle ancestor had built in the wake of the gold rush era in Paradise Valley that had never come to much in the copper mines in Cowboy Point. She now lived in the old house alone, save for all of her ghosts and regrets. Maybe that made it easier to tell truths to a stranger on the phone who she suspected she had more in common with than she'd like. "The first time I saw Helena, I knew a call like yours would be coming at some point or another. She looks just like my daughter, Cat."

Jenny and Peyton had a lot to talk about, it turned out. They both had two sons and a daughter each, all named after places. All names chosen at the behest of Patrick or Lyle or whoever he'd been.

"I don't know whether to laugh or cry that he created two families *exactly* the same," Jenny had said, somewhat helplessly.

"I find I do a lot of both," Peyton had replied in the same tone.

They had talked quite a bit over the past year, until an evening spent on the phone with Peyton, who was living over in Dillon then, was something Jenny looked forward to most nights. Now it was a new year. It had come in cold and snowy, just the way people around here liked it. Peyton herself was currently in Bozeman, because she liked a short-term rental, she said. Something she'd picked up in her years with Lyle.

More important than all of that, though, was that the Patrick brothers were due in town any day now.

Jenny and Peyton had decided it was best to meet up, in person at last, in advance of that arrival.

She'd helped plan this meeting and yet Jenny found herself something like nervous. She hit the interstate once she made it down Copper Mountain and wound through Marietta, then drove up toward Livingston. It was a sullen, cold morning. There hadn't been much light to speak of in weeks, though there were glimmers of it today up high above the Gallatins as she made her way along the highway. Nothing more than that low smudge of pale light that marked a full winter daylight this far north.

Like most things, it was beautiful. If you knew how to look at it.

Maybe, she acknowledged as she closed in on Livingston, she didn't want anything to change. She liked these faceless, anonymous discussions with Peyton on the phone. Meeting in person felt a little too close to scary. Like they'd have to give up all those rambling, confessional, healing conversations if they actually shared a physical space.

But she laughed as she thought that. Because who was she kidding? They'd already shared far more than most folks who lived on top of each other.

She was still laughing about that as she made her way into sturdy, charming Livingston itself, hunkered down against the relentless onslaught of the early February weather. There was snow on the ground, but nothing worrying, and none coming down as she parked. The famous wind was up to its usual nonsense this morning—she could see it causing a commotion wherever it found a sign or a stray tree branch—so she raced from her parking space in a bent-over attempt to keep it from slicing her in half, then threw herself into the coffee shop where she and Peyton were supposed to meet. And it took a minute to wrestle the door shut behind her.

It was warm inside, bright and cheery with music playing, the hum of conversation, and the louder *whir* of the espresso machine. She stopped just inside the door and unzipped her coat to let the warmth in quicker. Then she pulled her knit hat off of her head, running a hand through her hair to get the static out.

As she was doing that, she glanced around the tables where people were sitting in casual, small groups, not sure how she was expected to recognize a woman who was a stranger to her despite all the things they shared—

But then she stopped, and stared.

And the woman staring back at her had the same look on her face that she expected was on hers.

Arrested. *Astonished.*

There was one beat. Another.

And then they both laughed.

It was a helpless, whole-body laughter, and Jenny staggered over to the table to sit down and keep on laughing, because it was that or end up on the creaky wood floor. They laughed and laughed and kept on laughing.

In the end, they were wiping at their eyes, still laughing, and looking at each other as if they were about to speak, but laughing again instead.

Jenny imagined that at least half the coffee shop was staring at them, but she couldn't let herself care about something like that. It was one more reason they'd chosen neutral ground for this. Space to react however they wanted.

It took a good long while, but finally, they subsided. They were both sniffling and wiping at their eyes, and Jenny's face and belly actually hurt from all of that laughing.

It occurred to her that maybe it had been a while since she'd laughed so much. And certainly it had been a lifetime since she'd laughed at anything for this long.

Eventually, they both settled back in their chairs. They looked across the table at each other, and took each other's measure. This time without the laughter.

The thing was… it was like looking in a mirror.

More or less.

"Well," Jenny said after a moment. "There's no mistaking it."

"Indeed there isn't," replied the woman across from her, who could be no one but Peyton Patrick. She shook her head. "I guess he had a type."

Jenny couldn't believe it. And yet… she could. "We could be sisters."

"At least we can be assured that he had good taste," Peyton said, her mouth kicking up in one corner. "That makes me happier than I expected to feel in a moment like this."

It was true. They really could have been sisters. Jenny's hair was redder. Peyton's was blacker. They both wore it long. Peyton also had blue eyes that Jenny could confuse for her own. Blue eyes that all of their children were known for, come to that.

They were even shaped the same, for the most part. She thought Peyton was a bit taller, with her dark hair below her shoulders while Jenny's hit midshoulder, but they had the same basic lines.

In the aftermath of all that laughter, as they both sat there in silence for a moment or two, Jenny assumed that they were both letting the implications take hold.

Peyton rubbed at her face again, managing to sort out her eyeliner in two quick movements of her fingers, indicating that she spent more time wearing makeup than Jenny ever had. Maybe that was the only other immediately apparent difference between them.

Her head was spinning a bit, so Jenny took the opportunity to go and get herself a coffee concoction that promised to give her an entirely new personality, and possibly a heart attack, so she grabbed a few pastries just to be sure.

Then she came back to the table and settled down with this woman who she supposed had been her husband's mistress… but did that really count in a situation like this?

He had married them both. It was true that Lyle Patrick didn't exist and the marriage therefore wasn't real, but Peyton couldn't possibly have known that. She'd told Jenny from the start that she'd had no idea until he'd disappeared and she'd started digging around and had found nothing but… Patrick Lisle, Cowboy Point, and a wife and family that predated her, to her horror.

Jenny also hadn't had the slightest idea that Patrick had been out there with a whole other family. Other women, sure. That tracked. But an entire second family? From the man who had seemed to find the one family so overwhelming?

She still found it hard to get her head around.

"My older two are determined to settle in Cowboy Point for a while and see what it's all about," Peyton said, picking at the gigantic almond croissant that Jenny had brought over to the table for them to share. "They would tell you that they're going to see what kind of mess Helena's made of it all, but I don't know if that's true. They'd never admit it, but I think they do really want to know the other side of their family. I can't really blame them."

But she didn't look at Jenny when she said that. Allowing Jenny to assign blame, perhaps. Or have to arrange her face to avoid looking like that was what she was doing. It was sweet, but Jenny didn't need it.

"No," she agreed at once. "I don't blame them either. There's only one person to blame, and he never was any good at taking responsibility for anything, so that's a dead end." She made a face. "No pun intended."

"Do you believe he's really gone?" Peyton asked, her eyebrows crooking up. "I keep expecting him to… turn back up again. Like the worst sort of penny."

"Part of me wishes he would," Jenny confessed. "I'm not the woman he left any longer. His children are all grown up now. I bet it wouldn't be quite the situation he might imagine." She shook her head, because this wasn't the time to air out all those fantasies based in righteous indignation. Not at their *first* real meeting. "But I have his death certificate." She lifted a hand when Peyton made a face. "I know, I know. I do take comfort in the fact that Patrick Lisle is legally dead, no matter if he really is or not, and can have no claim on anything he left behind in Cowboy Point."

"I similarly take comfort in the fact that Lyle Patrick never existed," Peyton said, her smile cooling. "So he'd have a hard time claiming anything that he thinks ought to be his through an act of what I believe is a felony in some places. People do tend to frown on willful and deliberate bigamy, last I checked."

"Of course," Jenny pointed out, "if he *is* still alive, we can be certain that there are at least two other women in this very same position right now."

"We know that for a fact," Peyton agreed ruefully. "Who knows? Maybe we'll be a whole big club before we're done."

This time, their laughter was a little hollow.

Peyton reached across the table then and took Jenny's hands in hers. And Jenny had never been much of a random toucher, but for some reason, she found herself holding on tight.

"It looks like we're bringing the family together," Peyton said, no laughter left on her face now. Just those intense blue eyes. "I'm not sure that would be my decision, but Helena has always had a mind of her own. She's very determined. And honestly? I don't want to add to your hurt any more than I already have, but I can't think of this as a bad thing. It was the last thing he wanted, so to me, it seems like a no-brainer to go ahead and do it."

"I want to disagree," Jenny told her, matching the intensity and honesty. "But I think that's a knee-jerk reaction." She didn't let go of Peyton's hands. "I've known Patrick since he was a kid. We started dating when we were fourteen. He lied to me then and I don't really know what made me think he would ever stop. I blame myself, if you want to know the truth." When Peyton started to argue that, she shook her head. "What matters are the kids. We both know the kind of effect a father like him can have on kids who deserve better. I can see it in my sons. My daughter is married and wildly happy, but she feels like the outlier, if I'm honest. Though, given who Cat is, that makes sense."

"I don't want our children to make the same mistakes we did," Peyton said fiercely. "And I'll go a step further. I'm prepared to do whatever is necessary to make sure that they don't."

Jenny caught her breath a little bit at that. Because she was sitting at a table with a woman that a passerby might think she was related to, and she supposed that in some ways, she was.

The truth was, she had never felt more united in anything. She wasn't sure that it was possible for her to feel closer to another human being, because what other human being could possibly understand any of this?

Patrick himself, so charming, so beautiful, and yet so empty inside. What it had been like to love him. To pour into him over and over again, and know entirely too well the difference between him when he was pouring back—and when he very distinctly *was not*.

She and Peyton had crossed that barrier on the phone some time ago. She didn't know if it made her feel better or worse to know that he'd been just as wonderful—and just as horrible—to both of them. Lately she'd been coming to accept that she might never know.

It really was a club that neither one of them wanted to be in, but here they were.

Putting aside Cat, who had found her perfect match already, they had five children on the line. It didn't matter how grown-up those children were. To Jenny and Peyton, they were still and would always be their babies.

And it seemed they shared that same bright fire inside when it came to their babies. Jenny couldn't help but love that about her.

"I don't know about you," Peyton said after a moment. "But my children are going to need a little encouragement to get their acts together. Finn, my oldest, has a responsibility obsession that led him to wasting too much of his life trying to be quote 'good enough' to buy some ranch land in Colorado that was sold out from under him anyway. Raleigh, my middle child, has a way with horses and a way with women, and I don't believe he'll ever settle down if he can help it. And that's a shame, because he has the heart his own father never did. And Helena?" Peyton shook her head. "She has the biggest heart of them all, but I don't think she'll let anyone near enough to touch it. Because I'm pretty sure she needs exactly the kind of man she thinks she hates."

"I can relate." Jenny was nodding. "Cat, my youngest, always had her eyes on the horizon. Then it turned out that she found all the horizons she needed in a man who really is a little old for her." She shrugged. "But between you and me, I don't think this younger generation understands that sometimes, what a girl wants is a grown man, not a boy."

"Hear, hear," murmured Peyton.

"Tennessee thinks he needs to control the world as the oldest son and the so-called head of the family," Jenny continued. "And, I have to say, he's good at it. But still. I worry that it will all calcify in him. Meanwhile, Dallas had an early marriage while he was still in the military that somehow went awry, though he'll never speak of it, and he's been tilting at windmills ever since. Literally. He's been renovating an old lighthouse—"

"I've heard about this lighthouse," Peyton said with a grin. "In the middle of the Rocky Mountains with no water in sight."

Jenny nodded. "I don't know what he'll do when it's finished. I think he's living for the project and very little else."

"Well, I have a better project for us," Peyton declared. "And indirectly, all of them. I think we'll have to facilitate the first meeting. We're probably going to have to make it clear that you and I are completely on board with the meeting and melding of the families." She waited for Jenny to nod her agreement. "And that we want to become the best and happiest family that ever existed, *specifically because* their father would have hated that with all that he was."

"I'm pretty sure that will win over the whole crowd," Jenny said. "But I want more than that."

"So do I," Peyton agreed. "They deserve better."

"And they're not going to make the kind of romantic mistakes that we did." Jenny shook her head. "Not even close."

"No matter what," Peyton agreed.

And then, still gripping each other's hands, they shook on it.

Jenny could feel it inside of her, like a vow.

And it was one she intended to keep.
Whatever it took.

LATER THAT WEEK, on a frigid Saturday that couldn't decide between snow and freezing rain, Jenny invited the entire Patrick family into the stately old Victorian on Lisle Hill. She made sure that all three of her children were there. She told Cat to come without her husband, not because it was a secret, but because this needed to be a family-only meeting that she was welcome to tell her husband all about when she went back home to the Carey ranch in the hills beyond their tiny town.

"Good," Cat had replied. "Because Wilder and I don't keep secrets."

And if Jenny had felt that there was some reproach in that statement, given the way they'd grown up, well. She couldn't begrudge it. She was allergic to secrets herself these days.

When the Patricks arrived, Jenny gave Peyton a big, long hug that was only partially performative. She noted that it was returned in kind because they both knew what they were doing here, and they were both diving in headfirst. Then she led the other woman and *her* three children into the living room.

She and Peyton sat together on one couch, another deliberate declaration of unity, and they both watched as their children looked at each other, and slowly—at least, slowly for Jenny's kids, who clearly hadn't recognized Helena until this moment—understood.

"Oh shit," Dallas muttered.

Cat swallowed, hard. "Um. The symmetry is a little disturbing, isn't it?"

It was, Jenny thought. It really was.

Tennessee and Finn frowned at each other, as if they were as thrown by their significant similarities as their mothers had been in that coffee shop. Raleigh and Dallas looked a little more quizzical—though Raleigh was more smiley with it, reminding Jenny of Dallas long ago.

Helena and Cat, on the other hand, looked suspiciously blank as they gazed at each other and—on Cat's side—finally saw what Jenny had understood on first sight.

"Is he really dead?" Tennessee asked, not shifting his gaze off of Finn.

Across the room from him, arms crossed in a very similar manner, Finn laughed. "Please say no."

"What we'd really like is to take Patrick Lisle or Lyle Patrick or whatever else he called himself out of this conversation," Peyton said then, with a little extra South in her voice just then. "We all know who he was. We know what he did, or we can surely guess. We certainly know how he behaved. But that only affects us if we let it. As far as Jenny and I are concerned, he's dead and will stay buried."

"And the last thing on earth that man wanted was for his families to meet," Jenny said quietly. "Much less get along."

They all looked at her, these six grown children who she suspected harbored wounds to match her own, but wasn't that the way? You did your best for your children and they still ended up with scars. There was no avoiding it. Still, she had to think that shining a light on these things made them better.

She knew too well that the dark only made them worse.

"Peyton and I think it would be a splendid sort of revenge if, instead of leaning into the sad part of this with the betrayals or even too close attention to the timelines, we step back from all that." Beside her, Peyton nodded vigorously, her gaze on her daughter. "We've spent a good long while talking about this, and we think that since your father clearly didn't want us to be a family, we should be."

"One big happy family," Peyton agreed, like she was making a toast. "In spite of him."

"We really can't think of anything better," Jenny concluded.

For a moment, the six grown children took that in. Then they shifted their gazes and looked around at each other, arrayed around Jenny's living room. They looked stiff. Uncomfortable.

It was only to be expected.

But then, as she watched, Tennessee—of all people—smiled.

"Goddamn right," he said, as if it had been his idea from the start. As if he was making it his. "We're going to be the happiest family that ever drew breath on this earth. Starting right now."

Chapter One

THE LAST THING Tennessee Lisle needed—or wanted—to see on his doorstep in the middle of a snowy February night was the chaos demon otherwise known as Matilda Stark.

Especially since she was holding a bedraggled, woebegone creature before her like an offering.

"Whatever that is," he said, by way of a greeting once he hauled the door open and scowled at her because she was not, in fact, a hallucination or a very bad dream, "I don't want it."

"It's a puppy," Matilda replied, frowning at him as if there was something wrong with him. When she was the one standing on his porch in the middle of the night.

Tennessee could see that the weather behind her had not gotten any better since he'd last paid any mind, which had been hours ago when he'd brought in more wood for his fire. There was a typical Montana winter storm howling down from the higher elevations, dumping snow and ice as it pleased, and he'd accepted that he'd likely be digging his way to work in the morning.

That was par for the course in the Rocky Mountains.

Besides, Tennessee was no flatlander, seduced by a pretty day or two in August and not at all prepared for the realities of life here. Tennessee was the oldest son and current head of the Lisle family—and Lisles had been right here in Cowboy Point before it had a name.

None of that explained what the disheveled, walking commotion that was Matilda Stark was doing on his doorstep. At all, much less at this hour and in this kind of weather.

He could see ice encrusted on Matilda's red braids that hung out from beneath her winter hat—itself a shade of livid yellow that would have hurt his eyes if he'd let it—making her hair into her very own icicles.

Knowing Matilda as he wished he didn't, he assumed she would think this was *delightful* if asked.

Tennessee did not intend to ask.

"Matilda," he began, though he didn't understand why this was happening.

Like everybody else in Cowboy Point, he was perfectly aware that Matilda Stark spent the bulk of her time rescuing animals. No one could avoid knowing this. Rumor had it that she transformed the outbuilding behind the cottage she'd lived in with her sister Rosie—before Rosie had married a Carey, which, given the age-old feud between the Lisles and the Careys, Tennessee was required to view as a downgrade and yes, he felt that way about his sister's questionable Carey marriage too—into some kind of private animal shelter. Maybe the cottage was a shelter now too. Maybe she had a zoo.

He wouldn't put it past her.

Matilda could often be seen driving around Cowboy Point in her ancient red pickup truck that no one could believe still ran. Especially the way she kept it stuffed full of animals, presumably more rescues. Though he guessed it made sense, insofar as anything involving Matilda Stark made sense, because she was some kind of vet. A vet *technician*, he was pretty sure, whatever that entailed. Or something like that—he couldn't keep track.

Because he did not need to keep track. Because Matilda Stark was not one of his endless and ever-increasing responsibilities. She did not work for him in the General Store that his family had rightly won from the sore loser Careys in a poker game in the 1800s, like his mother and his siblings. She had nothing to do with the old, fanciful lighthouse one of his ancestors had built at the top of Lisle Hill. She did not work in the family diner, because he could not tolerate anyone else in his kitchen, and also, even if he could, it would not be a strawberry-blonde menace who had once shut down traffic on the main—and only—road in town to allow a meandering bunch of raccoons to cross. Likely to raid Tennessee's trash cans, not that Matilda had cared.

Matilda was not a Lisle. She was not his problem. She was her own family's problem, though, so far, the entire extended Stark family had never seemed to view Matilda as the problem in need of solving she clearly was. Likely because she, unlike some of her cousins, wasn't exactly likely to throw a punch in a bar or get a little too rowdy on a weekend night, so her offenses were viewed as *cute*.

But Matilda and her *cuteness* had nothing to do with him. That he had occasion to tell himself this more often than he should have was its own problem, but not one he could solve at 12:17 am on a nasty little February night.

Which brought him back to really not wanting to know what she thought she was doing on his front porch. Or why she was holding out a puppy before her like a gift.

"I don't care what it is," he told her shortly. "Puppy, kitten, wombat—why is it here? Why are *you* here?"

"I rescued him from beneath the General Store porch," Matilda told him in that matter-of-fact way that he always found… unsettling. Because she was so otherwise ditzy, he assured himself. It was always a surprise that when she actually spoke to someone, there was nothing flighty about her at all. On the contrary. "There are at least two more. I need you to keep him warm while I dig them out. And, obviously, there are no wombats in Montana."

She shoved the squirming, bedraggled bundle at him as if she fully expected him to accept it. He did not. He would not.

But his body betrayed him. It acted on reflex—that was the only explanation he could come up with.

And the next thing he knew he was holding said bundle of bedraggled wet fur and Matilda Stark was disappearing, clomping down off of his porch and tossing herself back into the snowy, wet, entirely too cold night.

Giving no indication that she intended to return and reclaim the creature she'd thrust at him.

Tennessee was outraged.

But he was also, despite how he liked to behave half the time—according to his family—not a monster. He looked down at the tiny, wet, shivering little thing with big brown eyes that stared up at him. He could feel the way it shivered in his arms. He could see how tragic and woeful it was.

So he muttered a series of curses as he went back inside and started pulling towels out, so that when Matilda inevitably returned—because he didn't think she ever said things she didn't mean and he was pretty sure she had indicated she would come back—he would be ready. He threw another log on his fire to get it roaring again. Then he wrapped the shivering little puppy in a fluffy towel, held him in the crook of his arm, and waited to see if the little guy would get warm.

He also watched the clock. He decided that he would give her ten minutes. If in ten minutes she wasn't back, he was going to have to go out there and help her, because she shouldn't be out in this weather in the first place. No one should be out in this weather. It was the kind of weather folks avoided until it passed, something even a committed maker of unnecessary problems like Matilda Stark should have known as well as he did. She had also been born here, to another family that had been right here in this tiny valley on the backside of Copper Mountain for generations.

Besides, it was after midnight on a Tuesday. He couldn't imagine what the hell she thought she was doing out there, wandering around looking for beleaguered animals in a storm.

It was, of course, a very Matilda thing to be doing.

Everyone knew that, the same way everyone knew that if

you had a secret in this town, you'd better steer clear of the Sheens who owned the feed store, the pastor and his wife, and Zeke Carey—who was so genial that even Tennessee sometimes forgot he was a Carey.

Against his will, with the puppy snoozing in his arms in a racket of tiny little snores, Tennessee found himself wondering what her life was like. Was this what she did to entertain herself? Did she wander where she liked, poking around the wilds of Montana with this same recklessness, looking for animals to save without a shred of concern for her safety?

The obvious recklessness of tonight aside, he doubted it.

Tennessee didn't spend much time frequenting the Copper Mine, the only dedicated bar in Cowboy Point and a prime source of information on everyone who drew breath in the community, thanks to yet another purveyor of local "news," Shane Johnson, its grumpy owner and bartender. Still, he was sure he would have heard about her misadventures through the grapevine if she really did go to such lengths.

Whether he wanted to know anything about her or not. That was how small towns that were actually more like remote neighborhoods of slightly bigger small towns worked.

He'd never heard of her going out that much at all, which he'd always thought was because she really did have a job. The last he'd heard—against his will, because everything he knew about everyone in this town was against his will—the vet she worked for was down in Marietta. So unlike many of the members of this little community, she probably spent most of her time driving the treacherous ten miles up and down Copper Mountain that was the only way in and out of Cowboy Point. And was no fun at all in bad weather.

Matilda didn't have time to dip into whatever comprised the pool of singles around here.

Tennessee realized that he was thinking about singles, and dating, and without meaning to, *Matilda Stark dating*, and he really didn't like that line of thought at all. It made his ribs feel funny.

But he was also watching the clock, and at exactly nine and a half minutes, he heard boots stamping on his front porch again.

And he couldn't decide if he was pleased about that, or if some part of him had wanted to storm off into the snow so he could be even more pissed about this interruption to his typically quiet night of paperwork and not talking to anyone than he already was.

He went over to meet her at the door but she barged right in before he could get there, holding two more wet and squirming bundles in her arms. She didn't wait for him to direct her. Instead, she looked at the pile of towels on his living room table, then she toed off her boots and padded over to help herself to them.

In socks that didn't match. And if he wasn't mistaken, had holes all over them. He was sure he saw a painted toenail in a sparkly lavender shade that made him… unreasonably irritated.

Matilda paid no attention to him at all.

She set down one pup, then the other, as she shrugged out of her puffy coat. And left it lying on the floor, he noticed. Something he wanted to use as more evidence that she was a walking disaster of epic proportions, especially here in his ruthlessly tidy little house. But, sadly, he suspected she left it on the floor so it wouldn't leave a puddle on his couch.

Then she scooped up the puppies again and took them with her as she went and squatted down in front of his fire. She ended up cross-legged, holding them in her lap and cooing at them. Murmuring soft little words as she kissed them on their heads and used the towels to rub each pup in turn.

Only when she seemed satisfied with the state of the puppies did she look up at him again. And when she did, she frowned. "Your guy could stand to warm up a bit more too," she said.

Feeling simultaneously chastened and outraged that she dared chastise him at all, Tennessee found himself doing her bidding anyway. He walked across his own goddamned living room and sat himself down in front of the fire next to her with three damp bundles of mournful little puppies between them.

What the hell was *happening* right here in his own house where there was never any chaos of any kind, he could not have said.

"They all look pretty good despite being out there for who knows how long," Matilda murmured, but Tennessee got the distinct impression that she wasn't talking to him.

She checked each of the puppies all over, then handed each towel-wrapped bundle to him as if he'd signed up for all of this. As if he was complicit in her... whole thing.

He didn't know why he was letting this continue, but then again, was he really so far gone that he was thinking he might toss a woman with literal puppies out of his house in the middle of the night? In the driving, howling snow?

That he had to ask was probably answer enough.

Tennessee settled for glaring at her, but that wasn't helpful. She was still wearing that impossibly yellow hat. It was still blinding. Her icicle braids were melting, dripping onto the scrub top she wore, leaving a spreading stain of water on each shoulder that she didn't seem to notice.

He couldn't look away.

Not even when he realized that the long-sleeved shirt she wore beneath the scrub top was patterned and the pattern was mushrooms and foxes and what looked like ferrets with spectacles.

Looking at Matilda made him feel like he was losing his sanity.

"I wish people wouldn't have puppies if they were just going to discard them like this," Matilda was muttering. This time she was talking to him, he understood, when she lifted her head and leveled that frown on him. Like he'd mounted an argument. "Look at them. They're adorable."

"All puppies are adorable," Tennessee said gruffly. "All baby animals, specifically mammals, are adorable. It's how they stay alive."

Matilda lifted that disconcerting gaze of hers to his. Those gray eyes that almost every member of her family seemed to have. On her, they couldn't seem to decide between gray and blue, but they were always grave.

She didn't look away. Or blink. "Being cute isn't going to help them survive a February snowstorm in the Rocky Mountains, Tennessee."

Now she was talking to him as if she was a schoolteacher and he was an errant student, and he did not know how it was that she felt empowered to do that. *In his house,* which she had entered and commandeered against his will. He also did not know why he was reacting as if he wasn't older than her, significantly more responsible than her, and more to the point, *not* some close friend of hers that should expect her to drop in on him at any time.

He wasn't even sure Matilda Stark *had* friends. She never seemed to have any use for people. Only animals.

"Matilda."

He tried to sound pleasant, but that was a stretch at the best of times, and this was an absurd situation that needed to end. And quickly, because he had his usual early morning coming in hot.

So Tennessee tried again. "What the hell is going on? You have your own house where, according to everything I have ever heard about you, you have any number of animals at any time. Why are you here in mine instead?"

Chapter Two

Tennessee Lisle was maddeningly stern. He was effectively humorless in all social situations she'd ever witnessed. He usually stared at her like she was a bug that ought to be pinned to a wall and studied for deformities, and he stared at her a lot.

He was also quite possibly the hottest and most attractive man that Matilda Stark had ever seen.

Tennessee was a grumpy pillar of the Cowboy Point community. An obnoxiously good cook, who singlehandedly elevated that diner of his into something special that had tourists lined up around halfway down the street in summer. The head of his historic family even though he was not wizened and ancient like the only living Stark of the previous generation, Matilda's uncle Steven.

And, not least, he was an oblivious idiot.

Matilda had been head over heels in love with him for as long as she could remember, a personality flaw on her part that she had spent years attempting to iron out. To no avail.

Probably because she'd never operated an iron in her life.

Tonight she had seized the opportunity presented by a litter of sweet little puppies to approach the problem from a different direction entirely. She'd assumed that proximity would sort the whole thing out for her, the way it did in the books her sister loved to read and now sold, but she'd miscalculated.

For one thing, having this very up close and personal view of Tennessee Lisle cuddling a helpless little puppy was… not good for her nervous system. Throw in the fire and how close they were sitting and—

Yeah. Call it a miscalculation. Except add on a few more levels of sheer catastrophe to it, and that was about where she'd landed.

She had not expected to find Tennessee in gray sweats and a battered Chris Stapleton T-shirt.

Matilda was not *prepared*.

It took her a moment to remember that he'd asked her a question.

And it took another moment, but Matilda cleared her throat. "What would you have me do, Tennessee?" she asked, as if they usually spent a great many hours together, rescuing animals in tandem, which just happened to be an enduring fantasy she'd had for some time. "The puppies were right here. On your property. It made sense to come to your house."

It was possible that this was the closest she'd ever really been to him. Certainly in an unguarded, private space. They'd had entirely too many pointless conversations over the years, out in public where anyone could hear. Out on the main road that ran through Cowboy Point, or in one of the businesses, or at various functions over the years. This was a valley filled with pointless conversations.

Because everyone knew everyone in a small little place like this. That was what Matilda liked about it. She never felt any need to bother with all the pointless small talk because she already knew everything about everyone. It freed up time to do what she wanted instead.

This, she was aware, was not a popular view. It was one of the reasons people around here thought she was *a little off*. Matilda preferred it that way. It kept her safe from all kinds of tedious social commitments.

Interactions with Tennessee did not fall under that banner.

Most of her family were busy restoring the old lodge that sat on the far side of Cowboy Point, up on the far hill that faced Copper Mountain from the other end of their little valley. Tennessee had always been friendly with her older brother, Jack, likely because the two of them could teach unyielding stubbornness to the Rocky Mountains themselves.

Matilda had enjoyed a great many years of the typical crush on her older brother's best friend. But it didn't go away, and it didn't change, and it never felt silly no matter how much time passed.

She had decided that it wasn't a crush anymore. Love didn't stop being love just because it was unrequited.

But she still wasn't prepared for the full force of Tennessee's arctic-blue eyes as he gazed at her. His dark hair was always a little bit longer in winter. Which wasn't to say it was *long*. It was just that he kept it more closely cropped in the summer months, and she even knew why.

It was because he spent his days cooking in the family diner connected to the General Store, the two businesses currently representing the historic Lisle empire here in town. It got hot in the diner in summer, even this high in the mountains. Sometimes he tied a bandana around his head, and she'd been known to have a flight of fancy or two involving Tennessee as some kind of pirate.

Tonight, with that longish hair, and significant stubble on his perfectly shaped face, she was thinking pirates all over again… even though he was far too uncompromising and *strict* to be the least bit piratical. Her imagination could not accept that truth.

In the firelight, he looked as if he'd been fashioned from a warm kind of marble and brought to life. She was actually glad that there were squeaking little puppies between them, allowing her to do something else with her eyes. Her attention. Her wild reaction to him when he was looking at her like she was some kind of bold telemarketer who had thrust herself through the phone and insinuated herself in his living room.

That this was basically a reasonable summary of what she'd actually done here did not exactly make her more calm.

"Your house is barely ten minutes away." Tennessee bit that out as if the words themselves irritated him.

Or maybe it was the firelit silence between them that was getting to him, too.

"Look how happy the puppies are." She hit him with a full blast of the Stark eyes, a very serious gray tonight she hoped, which would allow her to look like a disappointed professor at a moment's notice. Like her cousin Sara Jane, the Cowboy Point librarian, she could fell packs of cowboys—including her wild cousins—with a single frown.

It had always come in useful.

Tennessee, however, seemed largely unaffected.

This did not make him less hot.

"This might come as a surprise to you," he said, and his voice was even lower and darker here than it normally was out there in the light of day, in all that wide-open *public* space, "but I do not live my life focused on the happiness of puppies."

She deepened her frown. "That sounds like a shocking indictment of your own life, if you ask me."

He did not have the trademark Stark eyes or frown, but the scowl he trained on her hit hard just the same. "I did not ask you. Just like I did not ask you to come knock on my door after midnight. And speaking of that, what are you doing roaming around town this late at night anyway?"

She would love to convince herself that he was betraying some deeply held emotion with a question like that. Maybe later, she'd twist it around until it felt that way. But the truth was, Tennessee had a terrible habit of acting like he was everybody's big brother. Even though she had her own.

"I was obviously out indulging in the wild Tuesday night social life," she said loftily. "As us single women are known to do. Cowboy Point is nothing if not a hotbed of romantic intrigue."

He gave her a look that landed somewhere between confused and exasperated. It was a look Matilda knew well.

But somehow, here in his house that smelled like him—pine and sunlight—she didn't want to hear the sort of cutting remark her cousins liked to make when she said things like that. She didn't really care when they did it. Or when her sister Rosie, who had moved in with her Carey husband and was awash in two sets of twins, rolled her eyes and shook her head with a smile. That was fine. Usually it made her laugh.

Yet she really didn't think she could take it tonight. Not from this man. Not from Tennessee.

So she kept talking. "Or, alternatively, I was at work. Do you really think that I'm likely to go out on the town in my scrubs?"

She did not find it exactly flattering that he frowned deeper at that, and then—and only then, she'd been watching him—allowed his gaze to move over her body.

It was worse than she'd thought, she could admit that. It wasn't just that he hadn't taken the time to notice. He didn't *want* to notice her. If she had to guess, she would probably say that Tennessee was deliberately unaware that she was a fully grown woman.

Much like her brother Jack.

But, of course, Tennessee was not her brother.

Though she was sure that there was something about the way his gaze dragged over her. Something that *almost* made her left hand pull at the collar of her crewneck shirt like it had suddenly become revealing. As if that little swathe of skin at her neck was too daring for a moment this intimate.

And she was kicking herself for her completely unhelpful and over-the-top imagination, but his eyes lifted and met hers again.

They were still just as blue. But they were different now. There was something gleaming there that felt the same as the heat from the fire against the side of her face.

She found, suddenly, that she couldn't breathe.

"You shouldn't be driving up the side of Copper Mountain in the middle of the night in February," he said, his tone completely devoid of inflection or emotion of any kind. "You know better than that."

But his tone suggested to Matilda that he was hiding something. Not only because she *wanted* him to be hiding something, but because she had seen him speak in exactly this same tone to his family members when she knew that he was mad at them.

Such were the enduring benefits of growing up in a tiny little community like theirs. She knew entirely too much about this man. She knew how he treated people. She knew what sort of grudges he held over time—he was a Lisle, after all, and therefore was never going to allow himself to like the Carey family, no matter that his sister had married one of them. And she knew that he was always there for his brother, Dallas, who'd come back from the military a whole lot quieter and darker. She knew that he took care of his mother, the way he'd been doing since his father disappeared for good when Tennessee was still a teenager.

Matilda knew he was a good man, and that had nothing to do with her feelings about him. He just was. Grumpy and entirely too gruff, sure. But fundamentally good.

She also knew what he normally sounded like. So the fact that this was different *meant something.*

It was just that she didn't know what.

So she focused on the protective overreach instead. "What do you think I ought to do when I get off work late and would like to come home?" she asked him, keeping her gaze steady on his. "There's only one road to Cowboy Point, Tennessee."

"Why don't you have somewhere to stay in Marietta?"

She kept her face blank. "Do *you* have a second home in Marietta?"

"It's not safe," he gritted out. "Especially in that death trap you call a truck."

"Her name is Clementine," she told him.

He stared back at her, wearing that confounded expression once again. Scowly and confounded. "What?"

"My truck. Her name is Clementine." Matilda sniffed. "Obviously. She's perfectly safe. I see to her maintenance myself."

"That does not exactly inspire confidence, Matilda."

The puppies were squirming a little bit more now, and she figured they were getting warm enough and feeling safe enough to remember that they were starving. She estimated them to be about twelve weeks of age, which was great. It meant they hadn't been nursing and wouldn't need that kind of infant care.

She shifted to put the puppies she was holding on the floor, then crawled over so she could grab her coat and pull it to her, and only realized when she was doing it that she was possibly giving a little too much of a show under the circumstances. Or just making a spectacle of herself in this man's living room that he had not invited her into.

But she couldn't really focus on that.

She pulled out a couple of the cans she always kept on hand in her big, heavy winter jacket, and then came back to the fire and cracked two of them open.

Tennessee wasn't even pretending not to stare at her. "You just… carry dog food around? In your coat?"

"Some women like weighted vests," she told him. "I prefer to stock up on wet food, because in moments like this, it's a lifesaver."

She set the food down in the little space between them, and all three puppies wriggled their way out of their towels and hurled themselves at the open cans. Matilda found herself grinning down at them, because really, what was better than puppies? Especially happy little puppies like this, who were wriggly and soft and adorable?

Long ago, she'd learned not to ask herself what might have become of them if she hadn't seen one of their little faces in the flash of her headlights. It made her too sad.

When she looked up, there was the strangest expression on Tennessee's stern face. She had never seen it before and yet something about it seemed to wind through her like a ribbon, a little too bright and strange.

"Look at them," she said, as the puppies feasted. She ignored how rough her voice sounded, suddenly. "It's amazing how little they need to be happy. How little we all need, really."

She wasn't sure why she'd said that last part. Rather than sit in it, she stood up and smiled down at him. "Is that your kitchen through there?"

"You can see that it is."

That was an unhelpful and impolite response, in her opinion, but she only smiled wider. "I'm going to get them some water."

She marched through his neat and comfortable living room and into the warm, inviting kitchen at the back. Tennessee had moved into this house after high school and the rumor mill had it that he'd renovated the place because he'd expected his high school girlfriend to marry him and live there with him. But that hadn't worked out, for reasons Matilda knew better than to ask about directly, and so she always felt she hadn't gotten the full story.

Knowing Tennessee, it was possible no one had.

But what that information meant tonight was that she knew that Tennessee was responsible for pushing out the back wall, and building a cozier space in the kitchen that looked out over a bit of decking that she was fairly certain offered a view over the seasonal creek that ran through here. And then married up to the river a little further on when it wasn't frozen.

Matilda opened his cabinets, which shouldn't have felt scandalous, but it did. She found a shallow bowl and filled it with water, and while she was at it, swiped the towel that hung neatly on his wide, gleaming, chef-like range.

A big upgrade from the diner, she thought. And wondered how that tidbit had never made it into the gossip mill.

Still, so far, everything in this house was exactly as ruthlessly uncluttered and clean as she would have expected Tennessee's space to be. That expectation was based on her observations of him, the state of the General Store on any given day, and how orderly he kept and maintained the diner over the years.

There was no particular reason that she should feel all that like butterflies in her belly, but she did.

Back in the living room, she went over to put the dish on the ground, and found herself laughing again as the puppies tripped over their own feet and stepped on their ears to get to the water. She squatted down and spread the towel out on the floor, and then smiled blandly at Tennessee when he scowled at her.

"They're going to have to go to the bathroom, Tennessee," she told him. Calmly. "I didn't think you wanted them to do that on your floor."

"I don't want them to go on my towel, either." When she continued to do nothing but smile at him, he rubbed a hand over his face. "Matilda. For the love of God. You can't just come into someone's house like a wrecking ball—"

"Puppies are a gift, not a wrecking ball." She shook her head at him, as if he'd disappointed her. When really, she was going to be thinking about those sweatpants and the acres of unshaven jaw for a lifetime or two. She had to force herself to stand up again. "If you can just keep them overnight, I'll pick them up in the morning and take them down to the vet in Marietta."

"You're not leaving three puppies here."

"You used to have a dog," she reminded him, and only after she said that did it cross her mind that it was a potentially stalkery, psychotic piece of information to have right there at her fingertips. "When you were in high school. He went everywhere with you."

But maybe he just gave her the small town out on that one, because he didn't seem to react to the fact she... just knew his family pet situation.

"I haven't been in high school for some time now," Tennessee said instead, each syllable *deliberate* in a way that indicated that he was past exasperated and working toward pissed off.

Definitely time for her to leave.

Matilda moved over to swipe her coat off the floor and shrugged it on. "Here's the situation. If I bring them home with me I have a lot of other animals around, and I don't want to risk giving them parasites, worms, and any number of infections or diseases they might be carrying. It's not that I can't create a quarantine, but it would be so helpful if you could just watch them overnight. That's all."

"You do know that I open the diner at five every morning, right? A few short hours from now? But you want me to stay up with these puppies instead?"

"It's one night," Matilda said, with a smile he did not appear to appreciate. "And besides, I'll pick them up before work, which is at nine. So you won't have them that long. But I promise you, if they make a mess of your tidy little house, I'll clean it up myself. Deal?"

One of the puppies crawled into his lap. Another was

gnawing on the cuff of his sweatpants. The third was chewing her own tail, curled up against the side of his leg.

She would have taken a picture if she didn't think he'd explode if she tried.

He stared at her. "I keep thinking that this is a nightmare that I'll wake up from at any moment."

She laughed at him. He didn't like that either. She saw something a lot like temper flare in his blue gaze. "Well, Tennessee, if that's the worst nightmare you have going—three adorable puppies who might kiss you to death in the night—I think you're doing pretty well."

She was over to the front door now, where he had a neat little area set aside for the inevitable wet and muddy boots and snow gear, because of course he did. It only took a moment or two to stamp her feet back into her boots. And to place the other three cans of food she was carrying on the rough-hewn bench against the wall.

"Matilda," Tennessee said, in a warning sort of voice.

"Besides, look at that," she replied, as if he hadn't spoken. Much less said her name like that, all *growly*. She jutted her chin at the little trio, all curled up in a ball now. They were already fast asleep—two seconds later—full of food and blissed out on the heat from the fire. "How can I possibly disturb them?"

"Matilda."

"Thank you, Tennessee," she said, making her gaze solemn and intense. Or more so than usual. "You really are everyone's favorite hometown hero."

And then, because a storm was gathering on his face and

she expected it to burst free at any moment, she turned and let herself back out into the snowy night.

Then found herself grinning like a fool, all the way home.

Chapter Three

TENNESSEE DID NOT appreciate disruptions to the strict way he ordered his life—not because, as had been suggested by his siblings on numerous occasions, he was a control freak. But because an ordered life worked like clockwork, and he preferred it that way.

His childhood had been a tightrope of anxiety and spontaneous combustion, to his mind, and he saw no reason to live that way now that he was an adult and could arrange things the way he liked. The diner opened early every weekday and closed in the afternoon. He only kept it open all day and into the evening on the weekends.

And his entire life revolved around the diner. He liked it that way.

The diner was a known entity. The same regulars showed up every morning. He cooked the same things from the same menu that he had no intention of changing. He kept the same schedule that they could all set their watches to, and he never varied it, unless it was summer—when they all were so busy soaking in all of that daylight that all bets were off.

His life was a smooth, well-oiled machine. Some called it a rut, but he didn't care what his brother and sister thought.

He was the one who remembered their childhood the clearest and *he* called it a relief.

Tennessee did not sleep much at all that night, which was definitely neither smooth nor well-oiled. And he blamed Matilda Stark as every wide-awake minute of the night ticked past.

It wasn't as if the puppies weren't adorable. Of course they were. That was their job.

He considered rounding them up and locking them away in a bathroom to see if he could get an hour or two of uninterrupted rest that way, but he couldn't bring himself to do it. They weren't much more than babies and he couldn't bring himself to let them feel scared. He knew he wouldn't be able to ignore it if they cried.

So instead, he stretched out with the three of them beside the fire, and soon enough, all three of the warm, snuggly little puppies were sound asleep. On him.

But Tennessee stayed awake, as amped as if he'd downed a pot of his own jet-fuel-like coffee, glaring at the ceiling.

He might not have had a puppy in a long while, not since he was more of a puppy himself, but it stood to reason that if he didn't take them out pretty much every hour on the hour, they would relieve themselves inside the house. One of them rolled off him, yawned adorably, and then popped a squat right there beside him.

Tennessee hadn't actually known he could move that fast, jackknifing up to his feet and scooping the little girl dog up off the floor. And then there was no pretending there was going to be any sleep, because there he was, shepherding three furry little babies into the cold at hourly intervals, cursing Matilda Stark's name all the while.

He was still cursing her name later that morning when she came breezing into the diner as if she hadn't consigned him to a miserable night. Against his will.

The row of locals who warmed the stools in front of his counter from opening to about 9:30 AM every morning went quiet—a rarity—and then started up again.

They had all been pretty chatty since they'd seen the makeshift pen that Tennessee had made for the puppies back by the cash register, since he couldn't leave them alone in his house. It was an oversized cardboard box with towels on the bottom, but the puppies kept jumping up on their hind legs and sticking their cute little noses over the side.

Even Shane Johnson, the cantankerous owner and chief bartender of the Copper Mine, went a little soft every time they did it.

"We already have homes for these puppies, by the way," Tennessee told Matilda curtly as she came up to the counter and stood there, one hip jutted out against the Formica in a manner that he… should not have noticed at all. "Just waiting on that vet check you mentioned."

"That's amazing news," Matilda said happily, as if she couldn't hear the temper that he knew was laced through his voice. When he could hear it his own damn self just fine.

He had half a mind to tell her what the old men, his regulars, had said when he told them exactly where the puppies came from and why they were in his possession.

A pretty girl doesn't show up at a man's house in the middle of the night and leave him something unless she plans to swing back around again to pick it up, old Carter Redmond said. Because he was filled with advice on his town days, when he was dropped off around 5:45 AM and stayed until his grumpy horse rancher grandson, Colton Dean, swung by again to pick him up and take him back to Lost River Ranch, out there in the far hills. *I think Matilda Stark has her eye on you, son.*

All of his cronies had agreed, with a lot of gruff nods.

Tennessee almost told her that, because he thought she'd react badly to it, and that might have been entertaining. He wanted to point out that the fact these grizzled old men whose lives revolved around getting the exact same seat at his counter every morning thought she was hitting on him *proved* how ridiculous her behavior had been, but he couldn't. Because he kept getting stuck on the fact that she was so *pretty*. Something Carter had treated like an objective, obvious fact.

This morning, probably because he hadn't slept all night, that she was pretty was all he could see when he looked at her when normally, it was what she was wearing and how she was wearing it that drew the eye.

Today she was in a different pair of scrubs. This morning they were a deep magenta color and she had that wild strawberry-blonde hair of hers in plump golden-red braids that she'd pinned to her head so she looked like she really belonged on a Viking ship. Her gray eyes looked silver blue when she laughed, particularly if she did it in firelight, and he hated that he knew that.

He hated that his body appeared to remember it in real time, like it was happening now.

A truth Tennessee didn't like to think about too much was that he'd always been perfectly aware that Matilda Stark was pretty. It was just that he'd managed to avoid the grand mess of her for years. During any odd conversations that he couldn't avoid, he'd always focused on the *disarray*. The wildly colored, ill-fitting clothes that made her look like she'd rolled out of someone's attic, dressed in their rags. The hair that was either in those braids or half out of them, sometimes for days. All the animals, all the time. Her distinct oddness, in that she never seemed to *care* what she looked like or what folks said about her. She only smiled at them and carried on doing as she liked.

Last night, when he'd actually looked at her—her *whole body* instead of just her truck from across the road or that insistent gray gaze of hers—he hadn't much cared for his response.

That he had one at all, and that it was far more intense than it should have been.

Far more intense than he wanted to admit, especially because he did not do *intensity* of any kind. Intensity was just chaos, only more pointed. No, thank you.

But here he was, in the sacred space that was the kitchen of his diner, and she had barreled in with all her wildness again.

Making *him* feel like a mess when she looked like one. If not quite as messy this morning—it was more the sense of a gathering hurricane she carried with her, making all the hairs on his arm prickle like they wanted to stand on end.

Tennessee told himself it was just because he couldn't remember the last time he'd had a woman in his house he wasn't related to in some fashion. That was all. He might have been the sort of man who prided himself on his discernment, but his body had a mind of its own.

Apparently.

There was no other reason that he should have found himself lying awake, little snoring animals crashed out all over him, remembering the shape of Matilda Stark.

Now he found himself angrily cooking up hot breakfasts for a pair of truckers in one of the booths while Matilda took down contact details for each of the patrons who'd claimed they wanted a puppy. Shane Johnson and Carter Redmond among them. He knew that she was making a list not because she didn't know where they lived—as well as their names and probably their entire life histories—but because she was making it official. So they wouldn't back out and even if they did, she might just show up at their house with a hard-to-refuse cute puppy in tow.

Everyone knew Matilda's guerrilla adoption tactics.

But Tennessee didn't understand why he was paying attention to the things she was doing on a level like that, so he blamed that on sleep deprivation too. What else could it be?

"You little sweethearts are in luck," Matilda was saying, and Tennessee didn't realize she was talking in that soft, warm voice *to the puppies* until he turned to look at her in what he assured himself was *horror*—and found her circling back around the counter to look down at the cute little balls of fluff.

But she was. She wasn't looking at him at all. It was like she'd forgotten that he existed, and he could admit that he… didn't like it.

Just like he didn't like it when she simply picked up a cardboard box and propped it on that hip of hers that he'd been better off not noticing. She grinned at him like they were in on this together, which they absolutely were not, which he'd been intending to make clear to her.

He opened his mouth to do that, but she was singsonging a farewell as she sailed back out the door of the diner, making the bell ring as she went.

And no matter how he tried to ask himself why he was so *undone* by a girl he'd known for her entire life, he couldn't really come up with an answer. He, who always had all the answers, couldn't come up with a thing.

"She'll be back," said Carter Redmond, grinning like he knew something. "Mark my words."

"If you don't stop with that, I'm going to ban you," Tennessee grunted at him. "For life."

And since he wasn't known for idle threats, that brought about the peace he was looking for. At least until the garrulous old man contingent heaved themselves off into the rest of their days. He wasn't sure what to do about his own head.

When the breakfast rush was over and he'd cleaned up to his satisfaction—which was to say, to a high level that his family had been known to call *obsessive*, but no one asked them to cook anything, did they—he wandered through the private passage to the General Store, where his brother Dallas had just opened. Assuming he'd rolled himself down the hill in time, Tennessee thought uncharitably, like his brother was still sixteen.

He wasn't, of course. He was a grown man and he was right where he was supposed to be today, but old habits died hard.

Dallas lifted his chin in greeting, but didn't say anything while Tennessee moved around him and into the area behind the counter in the store that served as the general office for the Lisle family enterprise. Or at least, the supplemental office to the one Tennessee kept in his house.

"Why are you in such a mood?" Dallas asked after a while, kicked back with a to-go cup from the coffee cart outside. The coffee cart that was now a staple, since Helena Patrick—*their sister*—had made the whole town obsessed with her fancy espresso drinks before she'd revealed her identity.

That wasn't Tennessee being grumpy, though he knew he was often grumpy. If that meant people stayed away from him, great. Less drama for him to handle. The Helena thing was just a fact. What he was surprised by was that he really hadn't noticed how much she looked like Cat.

Well. Maybe not that surprised. Tennessee had never had a fancy espresso drink in his life, and he also didn't spend much time studying women. Mostly, he cooked and he cleaned and he handled the books and he tracked inventory and he kept all the various Lisle concerns running.

He had no time for mochas or mysterious women.

So there was really no reason Matilda should haunt him the way she did today, like she'd come in last night and shrugged off more than her coat and—

You need to stop, he ordered himself.

He glared at his brother. "Who says I'm in a mood?"

"I don't rightly know," drawled Dallas, looking entirely too relaxed for a man who'd been hermitting in a deeply foolish Rocky Mountain lighthouse for the better part of the last decade. "Could be the way you're stomping around like you're hoping the floorboards give way. The way you're slamming everything down when you touch it. Or maybe it's just the force of our deep brotherly bond after all these years and I can just tell from looking at you."

"Great," Tennessee muttered. "We're talking about *bonds*. That's terrific. Maybe later we can braid each other's hair and read out a few select pages from our feelings journals."

"I thought we were turning over a new leaf." Dallas could clearly tell that Tennessee was out of sorts, because *he* looked like he was having the time of his life. He settled back in the chair behind the counter and treated his older brother to his best shit-eating grin. "After all, this is the new blended family model. We're all going to be happy if it kills us, Tennessee. Even if that means *feelings journals.*"

Tennessee rubbed his hands over his face. He was much too tired for this. Still. "In theory, I couldn't be more supportive. Truly. In practice, I'll believe it when I see it."

"That's a hard same for me," Dallas said with a laugh. "All kidding aside."

"Count me in on that," came another voice, and Tennessee wasn't sure he liked the fact that he recognized it immediately. Or that it... sounded a lot like his own voice.

He and Dallas turned, and Tennessee wasn't particularly surprised to find Finn Patrick standing there on the other side of the counter. The oldest of the Patricks, that put him between Tennessee and Dallas. And the truth was, while none of them were particularly *surprised* to find out they had half siblings, maybe—that didn't make it easy. It didn't keep it from feeling weird.

That didn't make it bad. Just weird.

Finn grinned, and Tennessee had to believe he wasn't the only one who found this whole family resemblance thing part of the weirdness. There was just *so much* of it.

He and Finn were just about the same height, though to his mind, Finn had *cowboy* stamped all over him. Not that Tennessee hadn't been called a cowboy himself—a title he was happy to own, born and bred Montanan that he was—but he didn't think he looked like he was about to leap on a horse at the slightest provocation.

Finn, on the other hand, looked like he might have cantered over to the store bareback. No matter the weather.

But aside from that, it was wildly evident that they were all related. They all had the same chins. The same blue eyes. Finn's hair was much darker than Dallas's and Tennessee's, since they tended toward a hint of their mother's copper. And maybe his build was also a little leaner, a touch taller.

It was wild.

"I can't stop staring," Dallas admitted, crossing his arms. "It's weird to have a fully grown new brother, that's all."

"Again, agree," Finn said in the same tone—friendly, but

with no small bit of authority underneath. He shook his head. "Not that it's a bad thing."

"Not at all," Tennessee agreed.

The funny thing was, weird as it all was and would likely continue to be, he meant it.

It had been less than a week since his mother and Peyton had dropped the bomb, gathering them all together in the old Victorian house halfway up the hill. It wasn't that much of a bomb for the Patrick side of the family, of course. Because Helena had been here the whole time, hadn't she? Right here, under their noses, and somehow Tennessee and the rest of his family hadn't noticed how much she looked like one of them. Like Cat especially. Now that he'd seen it, he couldn't unsee it.

Point of fact, it was so obvious that he had to wonder if they'd all been willfully blind.

"We figured we should start a kind of tradition," Finn said, not letting too much of a pause build up. "If the Lisles are open to it, the Patricks would like to institute a weekly gathering."

Tennessee might have been exhausted. He might have Matilda Stark's Viking braids in his head in a way he could not explain or seem to get past. Still, he understood immediately what Finn was doing with this. It was smart.

He wasn't really sure why it hadn't occurred to him to do it first.

Maybe he'd put that on the night's sleep Matilda had stolen from him too.

"I like it," he said. "What were you thinking?"

"I think it should be something informal," Finn said, with that grin of his that was nothing but pleasant, yet Tennessee found himself thinking about the fact that this man had been running a cattle ranch in Colorado that he'd expected to own one day. And that got him thinking that where he tended to wear his responsibility like a hammer, according to his siblings when they were unhappy with him, Finn clearly preferred to cloak it in a little bit of velvet.

"I'll take that to mean we'll leave our mothers out of this gathering," Tennessee said. Dallas frowned, but Finn nodded.

"Exactly. It's clear our mothers have a lot in common, and I'm glad they've spent some time getting to know each other." Finn moved his Lisle-blue gaze from Tennessee to Dallas and back again. "It's my opinion, and I hope yours too, that we might benefit from some getting to know you time that's just our generation's. To keep us on track with making sure we're the happiest family that ever was."

"There's never been and never will be a family happier," Tennessee said at once, making himself smile. A big, wide smile.

Then he kicked Dallas's chair when he stared, his mouth open. Asshole.

"How about dinner tonight?" Finn asked, his gaze gleaming with what Tennessee was pretty sure was laughter of his own. "That pizza place across the street looks good."

"It is good," Dallas said then, still eyeing Tennessee like he'd gone a little rabid. "If you haven't been already, you're missing out. Those Bennett sisters know what they're doing."

"You don't know Dallas well enough to know that's high praise," Tennessee said.

"And you really don't know Tennessee well enough to know that he doesn't normally speak this much," Dallas retorted at once. "So yeah. We'll rustle up Cat and convene the family. And I personally will dive face-first into all that family bonding."

"That sounds uncomfortable." But Finn grinned. "I'm here for it. Let's choke ourselves on those ties that bind."

And they were all kind of being dicks, Tennessee thought. But somehow, they all found themselves grinning at each other anyway, and that was something. Or it was the start of something, he thought. It had all been a little much last week, all of them stiff and formal and staring at each other in varying degrees of shock and discomfort across the old living room with its fussy, historic settees that their father had once tried to sell out from under them. Literally.

But that was the whole point. They had a unifying theme. Their father sucked. He'd hurt their mothers, lied his face off, had disappeared, and had been declared dead seven years after that disappearance.

No one missed him, as far as Tennessee could tell.

Therefore, the families he'd left behind would be best friends if it killed them. It was clear they were all unified on that. It was impossible not to think that this was a good thing, no matter how they'd made it here.

After Finn left, making that bell on the door jingle the way it clearly hadn't when he'd walked in—which Tennessee could tell Dallas was thinking about the same as he was, and filing that information away—they were quiet for a minute.

"I think I like him." Dallas rolled his coffee cup between his palms. "Though he's a little too used to getting his own way."

"Though, so far, using his power for good," Tennessee said, considering that velvet hammer again. "Not a bad start."

But he heard the bell from the other side, meaning someone had walked into the diner, so he clapped his brother on the back and got back to work.

He closed the diner in the early afternoon in winter and when it was all cleaned up, he headed out back. Tennessee trudged back across the little bit of land between the General Store and his house, taking the opportunity to breathe in deep the way he always did.

Because no matter how tired he was, he liked to take a moment to appreciate the Montana of it all—another thing he'd learned to do in opposition to his father, who'd made no secret of the fact that he hated it here.

Their family had been here in Montana from the start of Cowboy Point. And actually even earlier than that, according to the legends of the family. Ebenezer Lisle had tried his hand at mining wherever he could, but had settled here, winning the General Store in a much-disputed card game from notorious sore loser, Matthew Carey.

Lisles had been here ever since. Sometimes Tennessee thought he could feel that in his bones. Every single hard winter and the golden summers in between, one Lisle after the next somehow holding on strong.

He blamed Matilda for how intense all that history felt today.

He was used to not sleeping much. He'd learned how to get by on only a handful of hours. But not sleeping much and not sleeping at all were two different animals.

And he was irritated that he was thinking about animals as he walked into his house, into his living room that now smelled like the cute little puppies that she'd carted off—with his towels—to sort out medically, presumably at the vet down in Marietta.

Then he was really irritated, because he found himself missing those cute, round little bodies, all the heat they'd given off while they'd slept, and the way they'd stuck their little noses against him like he brought them comfort—

Damn Matilda Stark.

He made his way up the stairs and into his bedroom, where he stripped down and showered off his shift in the diner.

And he did not appreciate it, at all, when his imagination decided to come to play. It was doing entirely too much work conjuring up visions of Matilda before his fire wearing a whole lot less than she had been last night.

He clearly could not let himself go without sleep again.

Tennessee had a few hours before dinner, so instead of getting into his never-ending tower of paperwork, he texted his sister to make sure she knew she was expected to appear at dinner tonight. He then ignored her response, which suggested he should try *inviting* people to things rather than *ordering* them to attend.

Then, before he became a complete and total stranger to himself and started actually keeping a feelings journal that would currently be all about Matilda Stark, he got an hour or two of sleep.

When he woke up, he was convinced he was a new man. Or maybe the man he'd been before Hurricane Matilda rolled through his life last night and this morning. The man he'd always been, since back when he'd had to grow up fast and act like the grown man his father should have been.

He felt like himself, right when he'd been beginning to wonder if he'd been doomed. If Matilda Stark had crossed some wires in him that he couldn't uncross.

It was already getting close to full dark when he went outside before 6 PM, and sometimes he found that disorienting as the year took its time turning back toward summer. But tonight he welcomed it because it felt like a reset.

And he did not really want to dwell too much on why he felt he really, really needed that reset.

It wasn't snowing tonight, but the temperature had dropped so low it seemed to kick straight through him. He welcomed it, rolling his shoulders back in his heavy coat, and was glad he'd shoved a hat on his head before he left the house. He shoveled a path from his house to the General Store and down to the road every few days, and it was a little packed up again tonight. But he didn't mind.

He walked through the snow and then out into the main road, where folks maintained sets of tire ruts going in each direction, and didn't bother much about the state of the road until spring came to melt the snow.

Tennessee made his way across the road, waving at neighbors passing by, and decided he liked the bright glow of Mountain Mama Pizza as he approached it. He hadn't been the biggest fan of the Bennett sisters when they'd first showed up in town, but then, he was always suspicious of newcomers. He liked good ideas as much as the next guy, but new ideas tended to freeze over and die quick deaths in a Montana winter.

But the Bennetts had been here a good five years or so now, he thought. They'd been the first in a series of other changes—*glow ups,* his sister would call them—in Cowboy Point, though some of those changes were harder to see in the middle of a cold, dark February. He peered past the pizza place toward another one of the previously abandoned old buildings that had stood there in varying degrees of disrepair for years. And where, rumor had it, a group of college friends were planning to open a restaurant.

Farm to table, Shane Johnson had told him, having heard it from the gossipy Sheens in the feed store, in a voice that suggested *he* did not intend to darken the new place's door.

But farm to table certainly worked for Tennessee. The kind of farm to table that folks meant when they used that term wasn't diner food, and that meant there was no direct competition to what he did. That was a good thing, to his mind.

And hell, he might like a nice dinner from time to time himself without having to drive down into Marietta to get it. Though he'd reserve judgment on that until the new owners showed themselves, the restaurant actually opened, and they actually lasted through a winter or two.

He knew that his siblings thought he didn't like anything *new*. They were wrong. He didn't like to get his hopes up, that was all. New was great—but he wanted Cowboy Point to thrive. That was a good thing for everyone. A long line of failed businesses, on the other hand? That didn't exactly reel in the summer season tourist dollars.

On the other side of the road, he headed toward Mountain Mama's brightly lit front door that beamed out into the thick darkness. In the summer, their patio was hopping with live bands and folks sitting around enjoying the late summer light. In the winter, they kept the happy lights strung up no matter how snowy it got, because everybody liked a little cheer in the darkness.

Tennessee knew he certainly did.

He was almost to the front door when it flew open and then he found himself face-to-face with Matilda Stark.

Again.

Like she was haunting him.

And even more when she blinked at him. "Oh. Hi."

She sounded surprised but then she smiled at him, and the smile was so bright that it took him a moment to realize she was holding a carryout pizza box in her hands.

"The puppies are doing great and I'm sure that's because of you," she said, in that cheerful, matter-of-fact way that she'd informed him she'd be leaving puppies with him overnight, too. "Thank you."

But unlike last night, she didn't wait for him to respond. She kept smiling at him as she sailed past him, leaving him standing there in front of the door to Mountain Mama Pizza like some kind of statue.

A statue who'd been blindsided by Matilda Stark's smile, that was.

Again.

And Tennessee didn't have to dive too deep inside himself to understand that somehow, overnight, he had managed to get himself into the kind of trouble he normally avoided like the plague.

Entirely against his will.

Chapter Four

IT WAS THE middle of a frigid February and that was why it was easy to get a table for six, no waiting, right at dinnertime. Mountain Mama wasn't empty—and Tennessee found he couldn't really remember the last time it had been—but it wasn't as packed as it usually was when the weather was nicer.

Last summer the place had been overflowing every night of the week, and Tennessee had to think the Bennett sisters were probably as happy as he was that there was going to be another dining option here in Cowboy Point. Hell, next thing they knew someone would be making those excessive social media posts about the *vibrant arts and food scene* in this *cozy corner* of the Rockies, and they'd all be overrun with flatlanders and fools.

Even more than they already were in the summer months, that was. But wasn't that how it always went? If a good thing could be commodified, it would be—until it lost all its value. That had been his father's stock in trade, certainly. Before that happened to a whole community, there was usually the phase where the summers-and-holidays-only folks put down their part-time roots and started throwing their weight around in town meetings.

Which reminded him to check when the next one was, down in Marietta. Some people liked to call Tennessee the unofficial mayor of Cowboy Point, and he couldn't say he objected to that, but Cowboy Point was actually no more than a neighborhood of Marietta. A remote neighborhood, sure, but Cowboy Point still had a Marietta zip code.

Marietta also had a mayor—Chelsea Flint, who had once been Chelsea Crawford Collier before she'd married the very rich Jasper Flint, who'd renovated the historic train depot in Marietta and made it into the Flintworks brewery. Instead of Jasper Flint making Chelsea—a former schoolteacher—too fancy, she'd somehow made him a local.

That was real Montana magic, Tennessee thought. Meanwhile, up on this side of Copper Mountain, they had to wait and see what a bunch of college friends thought *farm to table* in a remote little community was. He kind of thought it would depend on what college they'd all attended.

Though Tennessee allowed as how it was possible that he was feeling a little punchy after the night he'd had. And yet another run-in with Matilda that had left him wondering if he'd been deliberately hiding himself away for too long, if a couple of perfectly innocent interactions with a woman had him *this* rocked.

He went back to brooding about his hometown, because that was far less dangerous a prospect than anything involving Matilda Stark. Most of the time, while he was certainly never going to win a Mr. Congeniality award, he was a huge proponent of Cowboy Point standing on its own two feet instead of in the shadow of Marietta. He liked growth and opportunity, he just wanted it to last.

Like the very popular Farm and Craft Market that Flannery Bennett had started that was now a major tourist draw. And once the Starks had the Cowboy Point Lodge fully operational and running, and Dallas opened up that B&B of his, Tennessee figured little Cowboy Point was going to be unrecognizable—but in good ways. In ways that were going to make the old folks mutter, but they already did that.

What every small town needed was the young folks coming in, or coming back, and bringing the world with them in clever, accessible, community-based ways. Besides, the more modern everyone else got, the more quaint and cute the General Store and diner seemed in comparison.

All of which the Lisles could lean into. And would. And because Tennessee was in charge, already did.

He shoved all that aside because when he got to the table in the corner, his two new brothers were already there.

It felt weird—yet again—to think of them that way, but that was who they were. He needed to get used to thinking that word, *brothers*, because that, too, felt like an act of resistance against their father.

The three of them shook hands all around, and Tennessee found that he liked Finn's calm, capable demeanor more than Raleigh's boneless, lazy thing. Or maybe it was more accurate to say that he felt like he related to Finn more, right off the bat.

Dallas came in next, bringing the dark in with him, but then, he could manage that in full summer sunshine. The man had made brooding into art—and, soon, a place a person could pay to stay at and brood with him. He shook hands all around too, and clapped Tennessee on the shoulder.

"Evening," Dallas said, by way of greeting, and then they were all sitting there with competing genial smiles, which Tennessee was pretty sure would terrify any locals watching—because the Lisles never smiled that much. He wasn't sure his mouth knew what to do with all this wild, impetuous curving.

Before anyone had time to comment on the fact that the girls were late, they appeared, walking inside at the same time. But not *together*, if Tennessee had to guess from the way they snuck looks at each other as they wove through the tables.

He wondered if he was going to get used to the shock of finally seeing how much Helena Patrick looked like his baby sister. Cat, like everyone on their side of the family, had coppery tints in her hair while Helena, like hers, tended to be much more dark. But as they walked in side by side, there was absolutely no doubt that they were sisters.

And if Tennessee had to guess, right about the same age, too.

Probably better not to think too much about the logistics of that. All four brothers were about a year apart in age. Their dad had been pretty busy, it seemed—though never at his real job, of course. Because that would have required actual *work*.

He reminded himself that he was not thinking about

this. Not on their first happy family night.

Once Helena and Cat were seated, both of them looking wary to Tennessee's eye, Raleigh rolled up to his feet. "I'll get the drinks in," he announced in a drawl that seemed to reference too many points West and South to commit to any one region in particular. "I think we could all stand to lighten up a little bit."

He took everyone's order and sloped off towards the counter, where Flannery and Indy were moving around with their usual focused intensity. The oldest sister, Kitty, handled the kitchen in the back.

"Welcome to the inaugural meeting of the LPL club," Finn said when Raleigh was back and seated again, and beers had been dispensed all around the table. He lifted the bottle in his hand. "That obviously stands for Lyle Patrick Lisle—" and he spelled that out, so everyone got it "—God rest his twisted soul."

Everyone lifted their beer, there was the clinking of bottles all around, and then they all seemed to settle a little better into their seats. Tennessee could see several sets of shoulders lower a bit. Possibly his, too. The music was playing just loud enough to keep conversations private at each table, and the longer he sat there with these people who looked like him and shared his DNA, the less weird it got.

He decided he liked it.

"I've been thinking about it," Cat said after a few moments of sitting and gazing around at everyone, which they were obviously all doing. "I think our mothers were right to not dwell too much on the past. I'd still like to know a few things, though."

"As would I," drawled Raleigh.

Helena sat forward. She pushed her dark hair out of her face, and smiled as she looked around the table. "I can tell you the part of the story that brought me here," she offered.

Cat smiled. "You read my mind."

Helena nodded at Cat. "I'm a lot younger than my brothers, so when Dad disappeared, two things happened. I was less sad about it than everyone else, personally, because I hadn't really seen too much of him anyway. But I was also pretty upset at how wrecked my mother was. Later on, it would turn out that she'd found out some things by going through his stuff. She didn't share it with us." She shifted her gaze to each of her brothers in turn. "If I had to guess, I think she was embarrassed."

"How was she supposed to feel?" Raleigh asked, frowning at his sister like this was an old fight. "She didn't know he had another family."

"We all know who's to blame here," Tennessee said, before it could blow up.

Helena looked at him, and Tennessee saw Finn glare at his brother. Raleigh rolled his eyes, but he didn't say anything else. He only slouched a little lower in his chair.

Truth was, it all felt so familiar that Tennessee found himself in a far better mood here than he should have been. They were basically digging up graves and calling in a good time, but he felt right at home.

Wasn't that something. And here he was not *in* his home, either.

"I had to do a family tree project in high school," Helena was saying, as if Raleigh hadn't interrupted her, which also felt like an old, familiar rhythm. "I'd enjoyed it well enough, though it was pretty basic. After I graduated, I found myself working at a coffee shop in Missoula. My life was fine, but every time I talked to my mother she still seemed so sad. So I decided to do a lot more research. It turned out, I'm almost as good at genealogy as I am at pulling shots and making coffee drinks." She smiled at all of them, a glint in her blue eyes. "Our father, in case you wondered, knew better than to submit his DNA anywhere. But his mother had no reason to hide hers."

"Grandma Lisle?" Cat laughed. "She never told us she did that."

"Grandma Lisle was not exactly the *bake cookies and knit cozy socks* sort of grandmother," Dallas explained for the benefit of the Patricks. "She was more the *pull yourself up by your bootstraps, rub some dirt on it, and handle yourself like I did* kind of grandmother."

"Cuddly," Raleigh murmured.

"Terrifying," Cat replied with a laugh.

"Well, apparently, she liked a little genealogy herself." Helena laughed. "That's how I ended up finding out about Cowboy Point. And the fact that Dad had a different family. You can find anything in public records, if you know how to look. When I went to our mother, pretty nervously if I'm honest, I thought that I was going to rip her whole world apart. But it turned out she already knew."

"It was kind of a relief and kind of messed up, the way

she tells it," Raleigh said, still sounding protective.

"There were some family meetings," Finn added then. "Emotions were high."

"How would you know?" Helena asked him, pointedly.

That got a smile out of Cat, and the two women looked at each other in an oblique sort of way that Tennessee couldn't say he liked—because it felt like trouble—but he was pretty sure was foreshadowing a good sisterly friendship to come.

"Our mother wanted to leave things alone," Helena continued after a moment. "*Let sleeping dogs lie,* I believe she said. Repeatedly."

"Sounds like she knows who she married," Dallas said, with a laugh.

Across the table, Raleigh nodded his agreement.

"I decided that sleeping dogs could wake up, maybe, and anyway, I've never personally met a dog that stayed asleep that long." Helena shrugged. "So I came out here. And I really only intended to stay for a weekend. I got a hotel room down in Marietta and I thought I would just drive up here, poke around, kind of see where we all came from, and take off." Her expression turned rueful. "I don't know what happened. The next thing I knew, I was renting a cottage on the hill below the Lodge and outfitting a food truck so I could make it a coffee cart."

"While also spying on us," Cat said, but in what seemed like a big contrast to the night they'd all gathered at the house, she was smiling.

Helena smiled too. "You can learn a lot about a person

by the coffee drink they order. Both when they're alone and when they're ordering in front of other people. It's not always the same order."

"She's talking to you." Cat lifted her brows at Dallas. "Mr. *I only allow black coffee to cross my brooding, masculine lips, except when I'm drinking pumpkin spice lattes instead.*"

"I choose to celebrate fall," Dallas replied, with great dignity. "If you didn't hate and fear joy, you would do the same."

"Anyway," Helena said, still smiling. "That's how we all got here."

"That's how you got here," Finn corrected her, gently enough. "I don't think Raleigh and I would have bothered, if I'm honest. We spent more time with Dad growing up. So there was less motivation to dig into his past."

Tennessee and Dallas nodded at that. "Understood," Tennessee said, with a rusty laugh.

"I decided I was taking off and joining the military when I was ten," Dallas agreed. "I didn't care which branch, just as long as it got me away from here."

From *him*, he didn't say. Because he didn't have to say it.

The brothers all nodded, and shared a long look. They got it. Their sisters had been younger. Safer. It had been different for them. There was a particular agony in growing up and trying to become a man when your primary example was exactly the kind of man you didn't want to become. Ever.

"But once Mom started making noises about coming…" Raleigh shook his head, and despite his lazy posture, there was something stubborn—and, again, protective—in the way he firmed his jaw. "We didn't know what the reception would be like on your all's side. We couldn't have her doing that alone. You know, in case it got weird."

"Now it's *really* weird," Cat said, grinning. She leaned in, putting her elbows on the table. "But here's my question. Or first, a summary of who we are." She inclined her head across the table. "Tennessee, the oldest, the least fun, definitely needs a life." She moved to the side of him with another nod. "Dallas, possibly limited in ways he refuses to admit, may or may not ever open that bed-and-breakfast—"

"I'm on track to open the bed-and-breakfast next fall, thank you very much, fueled entirely by pumpkin spice lattes," Dallas interjected. Loftily.

He did not speak to his limitations, or Cat's perception of them. But then, Tennessee couldn't really argue about his description either. And normally he would hear something like that and think that he *had* a life, it was just one Cat couldn't understand, because his supported hers and all that usual older brother shit.

But tonight all he could think about when it came to *needing a life* was that smile Matilda had aimed at him outside. And how it was still sitting deep in his belly, like a shot of very good whiskey.

Tennessee didn't have the slightest idea what he intended to do about that.

Cat waved her hand, still in the middle of her summary. "And me, the youngest. Got married almost a year and a half ago, going to school, planning to become a nurse one day.

But here's the question. How do we, with so little to go on when it comes to any kind of happy family situation, make sure that we're the happiest? As we promised?"

"Board games?" Raleigh contributed blandly.

And maybe that wasn't funny, in the grand scheme of things. But it was so ridiculous, and so *not* what this group seemed likely to do at any point. Plus it was delivered in that lazy drawl of his.

Whatever the reason, they all burst out laughing.

Even Tennessee.

And they all had the same goddamned laugh, which they clearly all noted at the same time—because they laughed even harder.

"I don't know," Finn said when the laughter died down a little. "Seems like this is a good start."

There was a group consultation over what food to order where they found, to no one's great surprise, that they all liked the same kind of pizza. So it was easy to go and get a few pies, and some side salads so folks could feel virtuous, and when Tennessee made noises about chipping in some money when Finn announced he'd pay tonight, Finn waved him off.

"This is going to be a weekly thing. You can pick it up next time." Then he looked at his brother. "And then we can start down the line chronologically, so everyone can contribute to this family-building experience we're having here."

"Sir, yes sir," Raleigh drawled at his older brother, with a smirk.

Tennessee went up to the counter with Finn and waited

as Finn gave Indy Bennett the table's order. Then the two of them stood there a minute, looking back at the younger four.

"Raleigh's not actually shiftless," Finn said after a moment. "He does like to act like it, though."

Tennessee considered. "Dallas probably would do the same if he could. But the military beat it out of him."

They ordered another round of drinks that Tennessee carried over to the table. And when he came back, he stood with Finn a while and filled him in on the Cowboy Point lore he thought any sort of newcomer or interested visitor should know. Like the miners who refused to leave Cowboy Point, the ones who went back down to Marietta, and the really crusty ones who hightailed it out deeper into the mountains, leaving their stamp on the area in markedly different ways.

He was talking about the age-old Lisle family feud with the Careys that Cat had personally ended by marrying Wilder Carey when Kitty Bennett came bustling out from the kitchen with her auburn hair piled on top of her head, holding two huge pizzas.

"Hear anything about that new restaurant?" Tennessee asked her as she slid the pies onto the counter. Beside him, Finn seemed to stiffen.

Kitty wiped her hands on her apron. "College friends, apparently."

"I heard that part."

"Four women, according to the rumor I heard," Kitty told him. "Maybe one of them a local? But that's unclear."

"As long as they're still going for that full farm-to-table, high-end shit," Tennessee replied.

"Exactly." Kitty smiled then, and the smile took over her whole face. "So absolutely no competition for you or me, friend. Delighted to be able to support this new venture wholeheartedly."

"One hundred percent my take," Tennessee agreed with a laugh.

Kitty rushed off back into the kitchen, where, knowing her, she was already plotting out a new set of recipes. She liked to switch up the special pizzas weekly—even in winter—and they were always shocking combinations of ingredients that tasted fantastic together when most folks were sure they couldn't.

Tennessee didn't make that kind of food. His regulars wanted staples and they wanted consistency, and that was what he delivered. Day in and day out, with some special hours and dishes in the summer.

That was why he liked Kitty. They both knew their place, and the role of their kitchen in the community, and they delivered.

Tennessee picked up one of the pies on its tray and was surprised to find Finn still standing stiffly there beside him. Looking a lot like he'd seen some kind of ghost.

"You all right?" he asked his new brother.

"Never better," Finn said, seeming to come back to life with a jolt. He smiled. "I think I just realized how hungry I am."

He picked up the second pie and headed back to the table, and by the time Tennessee made it back to his seat, he'd forgotten that strange expression on Finn's face. Maybe not haunted, really. Maybe more like he'd been sucker punched.

But it got swept away because the rest of the evening—despite the built-in weirdness of meeting your own grown siblings, though it felt less weird by the minute—was actually pretty great.

By the time they were ready to leave, they were all talking like old friends. Or new friends, Tennessee guessed. Either way, they all told stories about their various childhoods without anyone straying too far into dangerous territory. Not that Tennessee or anyone else failed to talk about what an asshole their father was, but no one dwelled on it. No one got deep.

It seemed that there was an unspoken agreement to keep it all light. To keep the night fun and bright and *good*.

To follow their mothers' lead and make this the happiest damn family around.

"Every week," Finn said as they all stood up and piled back into their winter gear. "The LPL Club meets right here and excuses are unacceptable."

"Who put you in charge?" Raleigh asked with a laugh. "I would have voted against that. Was there a vote?"

"No one's in charge," Tennessee said. "This is a fully democratic family."

"Is it?" Cat asked in an exaggerated tone. "This is the first I'm hearing of such a thing."

"I'm betting that like Finn," Helena said as she wrapped her scarf around her neck, "what he means is that the broader LPL family is a democracy. The formally established nuclear families, however, can expect the same dictatorships we've always experienced."

"I don't want to run your life, Helena," Finn told her, calmly. Always so calm, Tennessee thought. He liked it. He was going to have to think on this *velvet hammer* thing that Finn had going on. "I want you to."

"So condescending," Helena said to Cat, with a roll of her eyes.

Cat slipped her arm through her sister's and pressed her shoulder close. "Let me tell you a little story. It involves me and my husband getting together and those two gorillas beating on their chests and dragging their knuckles on the ground as if I'm not, in fact, a fully grown adult."

Tennessee could have argued that. He could see from the look on Dallas's face that Dallas was about to jump in himself. They'd come to a place of peace with Wilder Carey—or near enough—but the fact remained that the man was sneaking around with Cat. Tennessee and Dallas had simply shined a little light on the situation.

As any good brother would feel duty bound to do, in his opinion.

"If we have to be the gorillas in her story, let her have it," he said. That obviously shocked his brother, because Dallas looked at him as if Tennessee had sprouted a new head. Maybe that was what a lack of sleep and too much Matilda did to him. Either way, he'd said it, so now he had to run with it. "If it makes the family happier, she can call me a gorilla all day long."

"She will," Dallas retorted. "But I guess in your case,

that's an upgrade."

Raleigh thought that was funny, so the two middle brothers walked out together too. And that left Finn and Tennessee to make their way out into the cold, bitterly frigid night.

Though Tennessee didn't think he was mistaken that Finn looked back a time or two on the way, in the direction of the counter, where Kitty was talking up a storm with two of her friends. Esther Wayne—the deputy sheriff's younger sister who had some kind of podcast thing, according to Cat, which Tennessee didn't care about because who had time to listen to podcasts? And Juliet Cross, one of the newer schoolteachers at the elementary school.

But only Kitty was facing this way. Tennessee filed that away.

"I know where Helena, Montana, is, of course," he said as they all came to a shivery sort of stop outside the door of Mountain Mama's. "And I've heard of Raleigh, North Carolina." He looked at Finn. "Finland?"

Because they were all named for places. They knew that. Places that Tennessee would have said that his father had never visited, but now it turned out that none of them knew the first thing about their father anyway.

"I know you're Catalina," Helena said to Cat. "I looked it up. California."

Dallas shrugged. "Mine is not mysterious."

"It would be fun if it was Finland," Finn said with that smile of his. "But as it turns out, it's a tiny little ghost town west of Helena called Finn. Another casualty of the gold rush, I believe. That's where they got my name, and by *they* I mean that our dad apparently insisted."

"Because even when he was a tiny little baby," Helena said, her eyes glinting in the light from inside, "they could tell that Finn was more of a ghost than a real boy."

"You can tell that we really are a family," Dallas said, and he actually grinned. "You're all funny and you all kind of suck. So we fit."

Everyone seemed to agree with that, too. There was a lot of slapping arms and backs, and things that looked almost like hugs, but not quite.

When Tennessee broke away from them to wander back across the road, leaving Dallas to drive himself all the way up to the lighthouse and Cat to drive back out to her home on enemy territory out at the Careys' High Mountain Ranch, he was feeling pretty good.

So good that he was all the way up on his porch, nearly to his door before he realized that there was a shape that shouldn't be there, sitting on a porch swing he'd never used even once and now thought he was going to have to remove.

It wasn't a ghost. It wasn't any kind of aberration at all, except that it had no business on his porch.

Then it moved and it turned out to be Matilda, wrapped in a blanket and holding a bright cherry-red thermos that steamed when she opened it.

"Not again," he growled.

And all the infernal woman did was smile at him, ear to ear, those gray eyes of hers looking something closer to blue in the porch light.

"I told you I was going to come clean up after those puppies, Tennessee," she said, in that chiding way of hers that made him vibrate with what he told himself was temper. Nothing but temper. "Silly. You'd think I was a serial killer, the way you're acting."

"If you were a serial killer, I'd know how to handle you," he shot back.

Matilda stood up, draping her blanket over one arm and looking completely unfazed. She was not wearing scrubs tonight, and he was irritated that he noticed that. It was viciously cold, yet she looked perfectly comfortable, though she must have been sitting out here for a while. But then, this was a woman who spent all of her free time scrabbling around these bitterly cold and often inhospitable mountains looking for animals to save. If anyone knew how to stay warm, he supposed it would have to be her.

Tennessee really wished that he did not know even this much about her. It did him no good. It did not help the situation at all, because it meant he was thinking about her far more than he should.

"I don't need you to clean anything," he said, trying to remind himself to go with Finn's velvet hammer instead of what Cat had once called his *mallet of malice*, not that she was dramatic. "What I do need you to do is turn around, go back to wherever you came from, and stay there."

Matilda reached down beside her and lifted up a bucket. She held it before her with a kind of quizzical look on her face, though he found himself caught on her mittens, which were rainbow-colored and, unless he was very much mistaken, knit to look like unicorns.

Unicorns, for God's sake.

"But I brought my cleaning supplies," she said when he only scowled at her. "After all, Tennessee, a promise is a promise."

She looked at him with so much expectation, as if his compliance was predetermined, and that shouldn't have worked. He shouldn't have cared.

And yet somehow he was opening his front door and beckoning her in, just the same.

As if that was what he'd wanted all along.

Chapter Five

Seeing this much of Tennessee in less than twenty-four hours made Matilda feel a little bit giddy.

Maybe a lot giddy, she corrected herself as she put her blanket on the bench inside his front door, actually hung her coat up this time—because she wanted to match the tidiness pressing in on all sides, and stepped out of her boots once more.

She did not look at him as she did these things. She thought that would be a step too far. Particularly when she was pretty sure that he *really* didn't want her here. That it wasn't just more of his typical grumpiness, that thing he did while helping everyone and getting involved with everything and generally being indispensable. While scowling, though. To make sure everyone knew he was terribly fierce and solitary and *might bite* at any moment.

He was a lot like a rescue dog in that way.

And the look on his face as she made herself at home again was nothing short of… confounded.

Matilda had delivered the pizza to Rosie and Ryder the way she'd taken to doing at least once a week since the babies had been born at Christmas. They sat around in the living room in Rosie and Ryder's comfortable cabin, mostly on the floor. That was where Mati!da got to play with her rowdy little toddler nephews, Eli and Levi, who delighted her more every day. She also got to cuddle her sweet, brand-new, two-month-old baby girl twin nieces while Ryder and Rosie sat back, ate pizza, and usually shook their heads at each other a lot.

Like… *what have we done?*

Though they always did it smiling, and usually holding hands, too. Meanwhile, Holly and Ivy were perfect in every way. Matilda had gotten to snuggle them, and kiss on them, and then run around outside with her nephews, too, to burn off some of their endless supply of wiggles.

She'd gotten to watch Ryder Carey effortlessly prove what a terrific father he was, and it still made her heart jump around in her chest. Because Matilda remembered what it had been like for Rosie the first time, when she'd had those boys on her own. She'd flatly refused to tell anyone who the father was, and she'd insisted she could handle it all herself.

They hadn't let her, of course. Rosie had been so tired. Matilda and all the rest of her family had stepped in, keeping up a kind of informal duty rotation to make sure there was always someone on hand to help Rosie out. Without letting Rosie know, of course. Because no Stark liked charity. It was hardwired into their bones—and was probably the reason that they were all so boneheaded and stubborn.

Then again, what family that had been in Montana for generations wasn't? It was kind of a requirement to live here and keep on living here.

After dinner, she'd driven back toward Cowboy Point, driving right past the turn to her house. Because she'd promised to clean up after the puppies, hadn't she? She'd parked her truck by the General Store and then had wandered across the road to peer through the windows into Mountain Mama Pizza. Because she just wanted to *see*, she'd told herself.

If he'd still been there, which she'd doubted. Because when did Tennessee *go out*?

But he was there, shockingly. More than that, he'd actually been *laughing* as he sat around a table with some people Matilda didn't recognize from behind, plus his own brother and sister.

She hadn't seen Tennessee laugh that much before. So she decided she liked those people, whoever they were.

Then she'd gone and waited in her truck with a hot chocolate she'd made at Rosie's house and carried with her in a thermos, because Rosie always had made the best hot chocolate in the family.

When she'd seen Cat Lisle Carey come out of the pizza place arm in arm with Helena Patrick—interesting, she'd thought—she'd eased herself out of her truck, grabbed her heavy, wool blanket from the backseat, and had gone to settle herself on Tennessee's front porch. With her cleaning supplies in tow, of course. Since she was here for very virtuous reasons.

It felt like a kind of late-winter Christmas carol to sit there with the quiet of the night all around her. It was cold, but the wind wasn't particularly high, and she liked that. She almost felt that if she listened hard enough, she could *hear* the way the stars shined down. Bundled up, she felt as if she could have stayed outside forever, though she knew better than to try.

And then she'd gotten the distinct and extreme pleasure of watching Tennessee walk toward her in the dark.

He was surefooted, which was no surprise. He walked on the ice and the snow as if he didn't notice it, his lean, muscled body hidden away behind his winter coat, and the hat he wore tugged down on his brow. Not a cozy knit hat, like hers. But one of those wool cowboy hats that men around here wore in the winter.

She could feel her body react to that. To him. She was surprised she didn't steam up the front porch. Sometimes she thought that there had to be something wrong with her, that she could feel as intensely as she did about this man when he didn't seem to notice.

But that was the thing about last night. She'd spent all day thinking about very little else. She'd gone over every moment.

He *did* notice. She was sure of it.

He just didn't *want* to notice, was the thing. If she had to guess.

But if Matilda had spent any time at all over the course of her life concerning herself with what people wanted, well. She would have been someone else. And she had no desire whatsoever to be someone else, because she greatly enjoyed being herself.

Particularly right now, she thought, with quite a bit of

satisfaction, because his house smelled like him. She took a deep breath and then she padded over toward the fireplace in her socks, carrying her bucket with her. And without a glance in his direction, she set about spraying the floor in front of the fireplace, and everywhere else that wasn't covered by one of his throw rugs. Each of them dark and richly colored.

She got down on her hands and knees, and methodically, efficiently, scrubbed it all up. Wherever she'd sprayed.

Then, aware of Tennessee in her peripheral vision but not committing herself to look at him directly, she stood up and looked around the room instead. "Where are all those towels? I'd be happy to run some laundry for you. I'll bring the other towels back up the hill when I deliver the puppies to their new homes."

"You're not running my laundry."

She did turn and look at him then, and as always, looking at him full on took her breath away. He had shaved at some point, so there was no impediment—she could look at that remarkable jaw of his all she liked. He looked grumpier than usual, or maybe sleepier.

And he was looking at her the same way he had last night. As if she was completely off her rocker. The good news was, she was used to that look. She got it all the time.

"You did me a huge favor," she argued. "I want to do one for you in return."

"The favor you can do me, Matilda, is to leave my house and not return. Ever."

She'd been getting some mileage out of ignoring the

things he said and doing as she liked, and so she had a split second of indecision then. She wondered whether she should continue along that line. As it was effective, and to her mind, entertaining.

But instead, this time, she let herself blink. She let her eyes go a little bit wide. Not exactly forlorn, but not solemn, either.

"That was very mean," she said quietly.

And then she just looked at him.

She watched him… seem to be absolutely unable to take that on board.

Tennessee was still over by his front door. He had taken off his coat, yet was regrettably not dressed in a T-shirt and gray sweatpants, both of which she imagined would haunt her for years to come. Tonight he wore jeans and a flannel, which was a typical uniform around Cowboy Point.

Even his socks looked deliciously masculine to her. Thick gray wool and no visible holes, of course.

He pressed his palms against his eyes for a moment, and he looked something like tired when he dropped them. And Matilda knew exactly why he was tired, didn't she? That was her fault. She really should have felt guilty.

"I'm sorry," he said. "I'm not trying to be mean. I am trying to figure out how I've seen more of you in the past twenty-four hours than in the previous… I don't know, decade?"

"Good luck?" she suggested.

"It seems to me you have an agenda," he replied.

Matilda felt her whole body shiver into something like

alarm. Or wariness, anyway. She wasn't sure what he meant by that. Was he actually going to admit that he knew how she felt about him?

Did she want that?

She might have decided that her crush was actually love, no matter whether he loved her back. But that didn't mean she wanted to have a discussion with him about it. Especially when he was looking at her as if he saw ulterior motives stamped across her forehead.

Not exactly a time for tender declarations.

"What agenda do you think I have?" she asked carefully. Very, very carefully. "Aside from saving puppies, that is?"

"You tell me," Tennessee said. "I've known you for your whole life, I think I would have heard if you made a habit out of barging into people's houses, forcing them to babysit puppies, and then coming back to haunt them—pretending that you have the burning desire to *clean*."

"I wasn't pretending anything."

"I've never heard any stories, so that makes me think it hasn't happened." Tennessee shook his head, that blue gaze seeming to swallow her whole. "No such thing as a secret in a small town, Matilda. You know this. There's just the countdown to it being public knowledge because everything is always public knowledge, sooner or later."

She had the sudden, wild idea that she should just tell him. That she should… lay out all her cards on the table, because he was a Lisle after all. The Lisles always liked card games, historically speaking.

But if she told him and he turned her away—even if he

did it nicely and easily—she would have her answer. And Matilda didn't want that answer.

She preferred her crush and the possibility that something might come of it, one day. So there was no good reason to tell him about it, she decided. There was a reason she never played cards. She wasn't one to take an unnecessary risk.

The only risks she took were necessary, as they usually involved the welfare of animals.

So instead, she smiled ruefully at him. "Well, now that you mention it, I do have an agenda."

She sighed a little, as if he'd read her like a book, and then she went over and sat down on his sofa. Uninvited. Because this was all uninvited, so she might as well be comfortable.

"I wanted to talk to you about opening up a rescue right here in Cowboy Point," she told him, gazing at him from the cozy leather embrace of his sofa. It wasn't that crinkly, stiff leather, either. This leather felt warm the way she thought he likely did, too.

But she needed to focus.

The rescue thing was not a lie. Or not entirely a lie, anyway. Matilda had been thinking about formally creating a rescue or shelter of some kind for years now. Rosie had always been exasperated by the number of animals she brought home, and Matilda had to admit that as much as she loved animals of every type, she sometimes also wanted to simply go home. Like last night.

Ulterior motives notwithstanding.

And she'd thought a lot about talking to the various community leaders here to see what they thought, because everything in Cowboy Point was easier when you had the support of the heavy hitters here on the main road. The Bennetts, the Lisles, Shane Johnson, and the Sheens. These days she would add Dr. Ramona to the list, and round it out with the deputy sheriff Atticus Wayne and her own cousin, Sara Jane, since a librarian was the closest thing around here to a walking community bulletin board.

"An animal rescue," Tennessee said.

"Or shelter, I guess," Matilda added. Helpfully.

"Right. Or a shelter."

That wasn't a question either. Tennessee said it as if he should have known that was what she was after. And really, he should have. *Of course* Matilda wanted to open a place where she could care for all the rescues she found or was called to handle.

It was like these people had never met her.

"Although I think a rescue might be better," she said, as if he'd offered his immediate assistance already and was drilling down into the details. "Just in terms of how to set it up, and run it, and so on."

"And when you thought about animal rescues and potential shelters, I was the name that came to mind?"

She frowned at him. "Yes, Tennessee. Since when does anything happen in Cowboy Point that you don't have an opinion on?"

He looked at her as if she was unfathomable. But to Matilda that seemed like a significant step in the right direction, because it was a step away from *unhinged*, which was where she thought she normally came in with him.

Tennessee looked at her for a long moment, and she thought he was going to order her to leave again. Instead, he padded toward his kitchen.

She stayed where she was, sitting on his couch, not sure if he intended to come back.

Last night she hadn't noticed that there was no television in this room. Just the sofa, the fireplace, a desk against one wall—alarmingly neat, of course—and books. Lots and lots of books on shelves built into the walls, stacked neatly on his coffee table, and tucked into other shelves that were also side tables with matching lamps.

Suggesting that when she'd come here last night, Tennessee might have been hanging around his living room, reading.

Matilda literally couldn't think of anything hotter.

He came back in from the kitchen, holding two bottles of beer. He sat on the couch beside her and placed one on the coffee table in front of her. He held onto his own as he settled back against the cushions.

"You read a lot," she said.

And then, possibly for the first time in her entire life, she felt something like *embarrassed*. Anyway, she assumed that was what this feeling was.

Because she felt… silly.

She understood that was because that wasn't what she'd *wanted* to say, it was what she thought she *should* say, for some reason. And it was a remarkably dumb thing to say, because she was sitting here in a room filled with books. Books that looked well-read at even a casual glance.

"I do read a lot," Tennessee said. And then, happily, he did not wait for her to say something else humiliating. He continued on. "Tell me more about this idea of yours. I thought you already basically had a shelter or rescue or whatever behind your house. Maybe *in* your house, now, since you have it to yourself."

"Bold of you to assume that I don't have a steady stream of lovers at my beck and call who require the house free of animals," she tossed back at him without really thinking it through.

Though even if she had thought it through, what she wouldn't have expected was his reaction.

He looked… stricken, for a moment. She was sure of it. That was the only word to describe it.

Then he looked away. "Considering the quality of men in the area, I would factor that into the *collecting strays* part of your operation."

She laughed, surprising herself. Maybe him, too. She was sure she saw his mouth curve. "Well. Fair."

No one had really asked her about this before. People made comments about her *collection* all the time, but that wasn't the same thing. Usually they were making fun of her in one way or another, which she quite happily had never cared much about. Let them. But he'd actually asked her to tell him more. Instead of telling her he wasn't interested, the way she'd half expected he would do.

So she swiveled around so she could face him, pulling

one leg up onto the couch between them.

Matilda picked up the beer he'd brought for her and took a pull. "There are always animals who need help and I think having a more centralized location to bring those animals into could be a benefit to the community."

She might not have come here to make this pitch, but she meant it.

"I don't disagree," Tennessee said. "Especially if it keeps me from having to babysit a surprise litter." But he didn't say that the way he had before. There was still that curve to his lips, and something a whole lot less grim about his eyes. "No matter how cute they might have been."

"They were cute," Matilda agreed. "And they already have homes, which makes them even cuter." She studied him, thinking about the people she'd seen him with and how strange that was on a random February evening. Particularly when she hadn't heard of any reason the Lisles would be entertaining at this time of year. Usually, if folks had visitors in town, everyone knew it. She smiled, hoping that would make her seem less nosy. "You should have told me you had company in town. I might have let you off the hook with those puppies."

"Company?" Tennessee blinked. "Oh, you mean the dinner tonight?"

Matilda had grown up in a family of many ruffians, so she knew a thing or two about telling lies. And how one of the easiest tells was overexplaining. So she didn't. She simply *exuded the possibility* that she might have returned to Mountain Mama Pizza to, for example, pick up a stray mitten she might very well have dropped outside. That was certainly within the realm of possibility.

There was no need to explain that she'd gone and peered in the window purely to see what he was doing.

He nodded as if the vision in her head made it through to him intact. "Here's a story for you. You know Helena Patrick, right? She's the one responsible for the coffee cart next to the diner."

"She makes the best breve in Montana, in my opinion," Matilda said at once. "I would follow her anywhere."

Tennessee frowned. "I don't even know what a breve is."

"Steamed cream. Pure joy. Oh, and coffee."

He shook his head. "Have you ever noticed that Helena looks like someone? Someone you know?"

Matilda tilted her head a little and thought about it. Helena Patrick was mystifyingly pretty. She couldn't even put her finger on why. Aside from the sleek, long limbs and that effortless, *just rolled out of bed like this* look that was always astonishingly cute. Plus blue eyes and dark hair, a combination that was always hard to look away from.

Matilda was jealous of that sort of pretty girl, her sister Rosie being one of them—although at least Rosie spent a great deal of time working on the maintenance of her beauty, which made it more tolerable. Matilda, by contrast, was not *sleek* in any way. She was solid, because she needed to be sturdy if she was going to be picking up large dogs and other heavy animals and carting them around. And she was *effortlessly dressed* in what she rolled out of bed and found of a morning, but no one had ever accused her of being cute in that elfin, manic pixie dream girl way.

She had always been fine with that. And anyway, he wasn't asking about her feelings about the pretty girls around town.

"I don't think I've ever noticed that she looks like anyone," Matilda said after a moment. "Except, you know. *That girl.* Always an air of mystery and a trail of folks desperate to solve it."

"Well in this case, it was resolved." He tapped the side of his beer bottle, almost as if he was nervous. Or processing some kind of emotion. It was fascinating. "She's been here a while, but her two older brothers just came into town last weekend. And the next time you see her, you might notice that she looks a lot like Cat. As it turned out, my dad had a whole other family out there."

He said that matter-of-factly. But she was sitting on his couch with him and she could see the way he almost… braced himself. Matilda didn't think. She reacted the way she would if an animal in her care seemed to be in pain.

She reached over and she put her hands on his arm. "Did you know that already?" she asked softly. "I'm so sorry if you didn't. That must have been such a shock."

When he lifted his gaze to hers again, she felt it go through her like a lightning strike.

"I didn't know," he said, his voice a shade or two lower than before. "But I'm fine. It's my mother I would have worried about, but she's known for a while. And the funniest part is, they all seem… shockingly decent, despite it all."

"I'm not sure that I would have it in me to think well of

them, even though I know it's not their fault, what their father did," Matilda said quietly. She shook her head. "I don't really have it in me to forgive my mother for being her ditzy, hippie self, and I'm not sure she's ever hurt anyone on this earth deliberately. She's just selfish."

And this was another benefit of who they were and where they lived. They both knew all these details about each other without having to share them now. She knew all about his father's attempts to sell the General Store—the Lisle family legacy—and all of his many get-rich-quick schemes. She knew that no one had considered him much of a husband or father, and that he'd disappeared while Tennessee was a teenager. They'd found out later that he'd died—or they'd assumed he had.

By the same token, everyone knew Matilda's father had died too, but her mother remained very much alive, if inaccessible. She liked to call herself *Moonshadow* these days, usually dressed only in undyed, coarse sorts of fabrics, considered herself a *keeper of light*, and lived on a commune farther out in the mountains. The only thing Matilda liked about her mother, and *liked* was a strong word, was that people assumed Matilda was just as fluttery as good old Moonshadow when she wasn't.

It was an excellent way to do exactly what she liked without repercussions.

Tennessee nodded, because he knew all of these things. And probably more, because he was older than Matilda. It was a convenient shorthand. She'd always liked living here, and now she liked it a whole lot more.

"We all decided that we're going to get along," Tennessee told her. "My father pretty clearly never wanted us to meet. So our mothers are determined to become best friends. And the rest of us are going to make ourselves the healthiest, happiest family that ever existed, even if it kills every single one of us."

The look on his face was intense. More intense than usual, and she thought she probably should have dropped her hands. But she didn't, because she was only a girl, after all. And his arm had all of those muscles and was so hard, and hot through the flannel he wore, just as she'd imagined he would be.

She couldn't help herself.

But she did scold herself into focusing. "Do you think you'll have to kill people to achieve this?"

He looked at her, and it was like his features softened. She thought maybe he'd taken a breath.

There was no reason it should feel like she was holding hers.

"Actually," Tennessee said, "I think it might be less of an act than expected." He shook his head slightly, like he was baffled by that himself. "I was expecting the worst. But so far, so good."

"I look forward to meeting them," Matilda told him then. "And I have to say, I'm not sure how everyone else in Cowboy Point will react. An expansion of Lisles? The natural order will be thrown out of balance."

She was only partially kidding.

"If we claim Wilder Carey as one of ours, and that's a big

if, we'll outnumber the Careys." And that time, when Tennessee smiled, it was a real one and it was directed right at Matilda. It made her feel as if she was flying. "Not that I'm looking for ways to quietly win the feud, of course."

"Of course," Matilda said at once.

When she had to drop her hands and sit back and actually *force* herself to talk about animals in the shelter or rescue she wanted to start—when normally, she had to be forced to stop talking about these things—she held onto that smile of his.

And she tucked it away, deep inside, so she could hoard it forever, like the treasure it was.

Chapter Six

February stayed cold, got windier, and then rolled straight over into a blustery March with only a few hints of spring here and there. The northern lights made appearances, the bison down in Yellowstone had a little less snow on their faces, and Tennessee found himself on Matilda's doorstep one bitterly cold evening with the Milky Way bright above his head and no idea why he was there.

He was sure that he hadn't meant to come here. That had definitely not been the plan. He'd gone to the weekly meeting of the LPL Club with his happy new family, the way he had every week without fail. And the truth was, the more they all hung out, the more they really did seem to get along. Like they were a pretty easy group of friends instead of complicated siblings with murky pasts. He liked it. He liked *them*.

And when he'd walked back across the road after dinner, he'd found himself studying the porch of the General Store, like he was waiting for more puppies to appear.

None did.

Matilda had brought the three she'd rescued from there back into the diner a few days after she'd cleaned his house.

And he'd… told her about his family when he wasn't the sort to sit around and share much of anything. He still didn't know why he had.

It bothered him all the time, to tell the truth.

She had handed over the sweet little puppies to their new families with little care packages that she claimed the vet had put together for them, but Tennessee thought otherwise. He would have bet anything he had that it was Matilda who made sure the puppies had a little bit of food, a favorite toy, and a soft blanket, the better to settle into their new homes.

She had breezed in with the puppies, spent some time talking to their new owners, and then had sailed out again without so much as a glance his way. And Tennessee had found himself pretty grumpy about that for days now.

Like he'd expected her to sit down with him when he was busy cooking. That was obviously ridiculous. He didn't like anyone bothering him when he was working. Cat often said his scowl was capable of knocking interlopers back ten paces, no need to otherwise engage.

Still, he kept finding himself rubbing that place on his arm where she'd touched him, sitting there on his couch. It was like she'd left some kind of mark. Yet when he'd looked, there was nothing. No matter how it felt.

Even now, standing on her doorstep, he could feel it throbbing, like a scar.

He hadn't meant to get into his truck, much less drive up the hill. He'd told himself that he was getting a lay of the land, that was all. It was a clear night and he'd driven up toward the old Lodge that the Stark family had been renovating for some time now. It stood tall, proud, at the crest of the hill. Over the past year they'd opened a lot of the cottages that dotted the hill in the space between the road that Matilda lived on and the grand old hotel itself. There were lights on in a lot more of them now that spring hovered near, he'd noticed.

The real grand opening of the Lodge was slated for the summer. And it looked like it was going to be ready, after all these years. The Lodge was a holdover from a bygone age, like one of those stately old railroad hotels that were everywhere in the West. This one had been built far away from anywhere a railway might run, but that was the way it had been in the West back then. Folks arranged their whole lives around a dream and did their best to make it come true.

Tennessee knew that his father would have claimed he did the same, but Patrick Lisle had never managed to do so much as cross the street without hurting someone on the way.

When the old Lodge had been successful, or at least that was the rumor in town, it was because the Starks had focused on service, not themselves. That had ended with Matilda's grandparents. It was their sons who had never agreed on a damn thing and had let the place fall into disrepair.

Patrick would have sold it for parts.

He turned around on Matilda's front step with its sweeping view down across Cowboy Point, and over to Copper Mountain where it stood snowcapped and pretty on the far end. Beyond it, there was a smudge of light from farther down in Marietta, like the horizon was candlelit.

It was a clear night, but he felt foggy.

If he was a wise man he would turn right around, get back in his truck, and keep on driving.

But Tennessee had his answer on that, because he didn't move.

There was something restless in him, so new and strange that he couldn't name it. All he knew was that before Matilda had shown up on his doorstep the first time, he'd been perfectly fine. Now he was… not.

Not fine at all, and his damn arm kept *throbbing*.

He turned around again, knocked on the door before he wavered some more, and then waited. Inside, he could hear some kind of commotion and then Matilda was at the door, throwing it open as what seemed like a whole pack of dogs leaped around, barking enthusiastically. She scolded them, but in a laughing sort of way.

When she looked up to meet his gaze, he watched as she actually blushed.

And somehow, that set all the restlessness in him on fire.

But even as it did that, even as he burned, he felt something like home.

Because that was already the answer he hadn't wanted to admit he was looking for, wasn't it? That was what he'd come here to find out. And now that he had, well.

His arm stopped throbbing. Everything in him stilled.

Now it was all something else.

"Tennessee." Her eyes were a wild, bright blue with her cheeks so red, but she sounded as matter-of-fact as ever. "What are you doing this far up the hill?"

"I wanted to see what kind of zoo you already have going," he said, with great confidence, as if that had been his plan all along. And when she looked confused, he frowned. Slightly. "To see what sort of facilities you might need for your rescue," he clarified, as if that was obvious.

"Oh." She cleared her throat and stepped back, moving a pair of smaller dogs out of the way with her feet and grabbing the ruff of the bigger one, a squinty-eyed German shepherd that looked as if he would very much like to take a chunk out of Tennessee's side. "Then you'd better come in."

Inside, the house was cheerful and chaotic. Messy to his eye, but not dirty. Everything was a jumble of bright colors and haphazard piles. Matilda herself looked much the same. She was wearing extremely purple leggings and distinctly patterned socks, though each sock was a different distinct pattern. The sweater she wore featured an explosion of what looked like forest creatures in a variety of garish shades.

It appeared that she was either colorblind or simply liked all the colors, all the time.

The most interesting thing was that her hair wasn't in braids tonight. It was loose, and it coiled all around and past her shoulders like a cloud of strawberry blonde, gleaming in the light of her living room.

He thought it looked like some kind of halo, and while he'd accepted over the past few weeks that he for some reason found Matilda Stark confusing, and oddly compelling, he was forced yet again to face the truth.

The old men had called her pretty, but they were wrong. She was beautiful.

She had all that strawberry-blonde hair that looked like a very warm, rose gold. He wanted to bury his hands in it. Those eyes of hers seemed to change color at will. She had freckles across her nose. And Tennessee found himself wondering if she had deliberately spent her life dressing like a batty old woman with the express purpose of making sure that no one would ever realize just how beautiful she really was.

Because if all people ever focused on were her eccentricities, that meant she could wander around the town without a whole lot of commentary. And Tennessee knew from watching his remarkably pretty sister navigate Cowboy Point that a little anonymity was a good thing—that or a pair of overprotective brothers.

Matilda's sister had turned up pregnant, and then with twins, and that despite all her ornery cousins. Not to mention Jack Stark, who a wise man knew better than to cross. It was lucky for Ryder Carey that he'd had no idea what was going on with Rosie while he was away, or someone might have taken it upon themselves to teach him some lessons. Tennessee understood the urge.

And yet somehow, all along, Matilda Stark had also been walking around this pretty. How had he never noticed?

Yet as she buzzed around the living room—talking a mile a minute about the books on the shelves that she said were her sister's, ignoring the piles of things everywhere that she didn't excuse or even seem to notice, even the way she pushed her hair back from her face as if she spent most of her time alone with it loose like this—Tennessee had to ask himself if it was true that he'd never noticed.

Because he had always found Matilda… unsettling.

He always seemed to notice when she was around. Maybe his subconscious had been telling him to pay attention all along.

Well. He was sure paying attention now.

Tennessee followed her through the house, back into a kitchen that looked cluttered and lived in—but again, clean. By the back door, she stamped her feet into a pair of rubber boots and waved for him to follow her. The dogs stayed in the house. And he thought he saw a tuxedo cat peering at him from the top of the refrigerator, but he followed her outside as she tramped across the frozen yard into the outbuilding out back.

He followed her inside to a door on the side, where they were immediately greeted by a wall of sound.

"I set it up kind of like a shelter," she told him, seeming not to notice the din. "But I hate shelters, so when it's possible, I try to create pack experiences for the dogs. Some of them can't handle that, but the ones who can get a little companionship."

It looked at first glance like more chaos. But Tennessee was learning. He looked closer.

And he could see then that there was an infrastructure here. She had kennels set up along the far wall with larger runs in between, but the bulk of the space was where the *pack experience*, as she'd called it, was set up. It was all fenced in. Inside, there were about seven or eight dogs—one of them a magnificent creature who had to be part husky, with eyes that blue. He stood apart from the pack and stared at Tennessee, like he was sizing up the intruder and implementing a plan of action. Tennessee liked him immediately.

But there was more. Here inside the small building, it was warm and clean. He saw cats in some of the kennels in back and what looked like a fox in one of the runs, though it only peered at him suspiciously and stayed mostly hidden.

"I think you came to me under false pretenses," he drawled. And he could swear she jumped a little, and her eyes were a bit too wide when she looked his way, but she didn't say anything. He nodded at her operation. "Seems like you already have a rescue."

She grinned at him, and now that he was no longer blind to how pretty she was—willfully blind, he had to think—that grin packed a serious punch.

"I need more space." She said that matter-of-factly. Like it was obvious. "Ideally, I'd like to have separate dog and cat spaces, not to mention a wildlife rehabilitation area. And, of course, an adoption space where folks can come and play with their new best friends before they take them home. And I might be a crazy animal person, or whatever they like to call me around Paradise Valley, but even I know I should probably separate that kind of enterprise from my house."

She started pointing out things she thought should be upgraded if there was more space available, but he couldn't track it. Tennessee felt as if something seismic had ripped him in half, maybe into quarters, and then slammed him back together in the next breath.

It was like every blinder he'd had in place had been torn

away. Like he had suddenly seen every possible timeline and they all led here. To this moment.

He hadn't meant to come here at all. Or maybe he'd been plotting excuses to come up the hill since she'd left his house that night with her cleaning supplies and that patchwork blanket he'd half hoped she'd leave behind.

So she'd have an excuse to show up again and he wouldn't have to do something like this.

Something he shouldn't have wanted to do in the first place.

He felt that earthquake rumble inside of him again, no matter how he tried to resist it. Because he had to resist it. Because he should have known better than to come find her like this.

Because he understood that there were consequences to what he was doing here.

Even if he managed to convince himself that finding her this pretty all of a sudden was an anomaly, and even if he woke up tomorrow blind to her all over again, he'd involved himself in this passion of hers. And he knew that Matilda was stubborn. She was the woman who had somehow convinced him to lose a night's sleep taking care of a few puppies, when he'd never allowed a pet in his house in all the years he'd lived there as an adult.

But he knew himself. And he knew full well that if he didn't turn back the clock on his awareness of her, that meant other things. Things he wasn't sure he wanted to deal with at all.

Things he should have thought about before he'd

climbed in his truck tonight and headed up this way.

Because Tennessee wasn't the kind of man who messed around with women. And even if he had been, Matilda was most certainly not the kind of woman anyone was likely to mess around with. She might as well have had *forever* stamped across her nose like those ridiculously cute freckles.

He had never heard of her being with anyone, but there was something about the directness of her gaze. There was something about her unflappable practicality.

There was the way she blushed at the sight of him.

All of those things told him things he'd be a lot safer not knowing. Because if he followed that blush, he knew he had to be prepared for where it would lead.

"You have a whole lot of animals in your personal zoo, Matilda," he pointed out. "Does everyone know how many you're taking care of back here?"

If he expected her to look chastened, well. He should have known better. Matilda laughed.

Then she looked back towards the animals and propped her hands on her hips. "I think they're mostly happy here. I try to make sure of it." She blew out a breath. "But it's hard to convince anyone to come up the hill to meet them. Most of them would be great family pets. A few of them would be better off as working dogs and such. And I think rescues do a better job about that kind of thing than shelters, because you have more time to really get to know the animals in question and you're better able to place them in good homes where they'll thrive. Theoretically, I mean. If I could get people here."

He was thinking about the flush on her cheeks and wondering if that would be something that happened all over her body. And then, once he was thinking about her body, he couldn't seem to stop looking at the shape of her. All of the bright colors and the exuberant clash of fabric and pattern couldn't disguise the fact that she was built. She was curvy and looked strong. He'd watched her carry heavy bags of dog food and the like out of the feed store, tossing them into the back of her truck as if they weighed nothing. Matilda was no fragile, wilting flower.

She was the kind of woman that a man conquered the West with.

And even as he thought that, Tennessee could feel something seem to chime deep inside of him, like fate.

But he refused to be governed by anything but cool rationality, and nothing even remotely like passion. Because Tennessee was nothing like his father.

He would never be anything like his father.

So when his hands itched to touch her, he shoved them into his pockets instead.

"How did you become so passionate about this?" he asked her. "Rural folks tend to be less sentimental when it comes to animals."

"I didn't grow up on a farm or a ranch," she said dryly. "I did grow up around folks I thought were maybe a little too callous about the fate of their barn cats, but the truth is, I grew up in a sad house. My mother was mostly absent, both before and after my father died, and we pretty much had to fend for ourselves. Jack had to act like a father too young and

I took it upon myself to act like it was my job to raise Rosie, whether she liked that or not."

Matilda said all of that without a shred of self-pity. Like she was simply stating facts, and they had nothing attached to them.

But then she smiled. "Animals were what made me happy. And the happier they made me, the sadder the way they were treated made me." She shrugged. "You could probably draw some lines between my childhood and my feelings about the treatment of defenseless creatures, sure. Somehow it all led to rescuing them whenever I could, making myself a nuisance at the Crawford County Animal Shelter as well as the vet. And then, you know. Also my career."

"I think it's a good thing," Tennessee said gruffly. "An honorable thing."

Her eyes darted to him, gray again. Then she looked away. "Some people think that you should spend more time rescuing humans and let animals fend for themselves."

"That sounds like the sort of thing someone who doesn't spend much time rescuing anything might say," Tennessee replied.

This time, she didn't grin so much as smile. And her smile changed her whole face—which was to say, it made her so bright that he was tempted to forget it was winter. He could feel that brightness inside of him, flooding through his body, like gold in his veins.

"There are still a whole lot of empty buildings down on the main road," he found himself saying. "Some of them have land attached. I bet one of them would work for the kind of rescue you're talking about."

In fact, he was astonished to discover, he had one in mind.

"Sure," she said, and she laughed. And that, too, was almost unbearably sweet. "I don't know if you know this, but vet techs aren't exactly Montana millionaires like those Flint brothers."

"You're a Stark and I'm a Lisle." Tennessee thought maybe he was grinning himself, or maybe she was just looking at his mouth. That worked too. "I'm sure we could work something out."

Besides, Tennessee kind of thought it would suit him to have more Matilda Stark in town.

She turned around and headed back out of the barn, and he followed after her—with one last look at his blue-eyed husky friend in the pen, silent and still. Like he had high expectations of Tennessee and would be following up.

How a dog made Tennessee feel called out was a mystery.

Outside, it was dark in her yard. The stars were a bright mess up above them, a lot like her and her house and her dogs barking out a symphony from inside the house.

"Look," Matilda said, as they stood there in the cold, "I realize I did, in fact, roll on into your extremely orderly life with puppies, which you were kind enough to handle beautifully. And I would love to figure out this rescue thing with you. But we don't have to do this."

Tennessee frowned down at her because it was that or put his hands on her, and he wasn't going to do that. He wasn't ready to do that. "I like animals, Matilda," he said, reprovingly.

"I don't know if it's true." He stared at her and she shrugged. "If I had to guess, losing your childhood dog broke your heart and you have no intention of ever repairing it. Or something like that."

The accuracy of that was a little bit breathtaking. He cleared his throat. "Why would you say that?"

Matilda scrunched up her nose as she peered up at him. "You're that sort, aren't you? Growly, brooding, stoic, and alone. If I had to guess, I would say that the broken heart thing was pretty much your whole personality. Like the mysterious high school girlfriend. Right?"

That was such an unexpected sucker punch that he was surprised it didn't lay him out flat. Or maybe it did, because she started looking abashed as she gazed up at him, like her own words were playing back in her head.

"My high school girlfriend?" he heard himself ask, still reeling. Still trying to understand how she could have struck him so hard and in exactly the place he'd stopped even considering a wound anymore.

"I'm sorry," she said quietly. "I shouldn't have said that. I forget that not everyone lives in my head, and might not enjoy how direct I am or the conclusions I draw with absolutely no evidence, or the things I decide I ought to be able to talk about with impunity. Really. I'm sorry."

She shook her head, though it seemed to him it was aimed at herself, and then she turned and started toward the house.

And he felt…

Tennessee couldn't have said what he felt, but that was the thing, wasn't it? That he *felt* at all. When he thought he'd turned that shit off in another lifetime, when he was another man entirely.

Or really, as he looked back on it now, just a boy. Trying so hard to be the man his own father never was.

"Hey," he said, and maybe he sounded more stern than he meant to. He watched her stiffen, even as she stopped dead.

She didn't turn around. Her head seemed to drop a bit and he thought her shoulders tensed, but she didn't turn back to face him.

And maybe that made it easier, here beneath the tapestry of cold stars.

He found himself rubbing at his chest with the heel of his hand, as if that could make the pain dissipate. Or the memory of pain. Or whatever this was.

"Her name was Kacey," he said. "Still is."

Chapter Seven

THERE WAS SOMETHING about the way he said that name.

Kacey.

Matilda found herself leaning closer and keeping her eyes trained on Tennessee, because something about the way he held himself had changed, too. She thought that she ought to have felt some kind of jolt when he'd said it. Something like jealousy, but she didn't. Instead, she felt the way she always did when she saw a creature wounded.

She just wanted to put her hands on him and see how she could help. Sometimes she couldn't. Right now, *help* appeared to be the simple act of listening. And she knew she could do that.

But first she led him back inside, winding through the gauntlet of overexcited dogs and the much warier cats in their hiding spots, and then made them all lie down somewhere other than the couch.

Matilda sat and waved to the cushion beside her, encouraging Tennessee to sit down with her. He frowned, and she wondered if he was going to make a run for it. He moved toward the door and she bit her lip to keep her disappointment inside, because she knew better. Sometimes you had to let the hurt ones find their own way, no matter how much you thought you could help.

Then, in the end, all he was doing was shrugging out of his jacket and taking off his boots, lining them up neatly in the entryway where she'd kicked hers aside.

A little Tennessee detail that made her throat feel tight.

"Kacey and I dated from the moment we hit middle school," Tennessee told her when he came back to the couch and sat down, then turned to face her so slowly that she wondered if it actually caused him pain to open up. "Not that it was really *dating* in the beginning. She lived down in Marietta and we only saw each other in school. I'm pretty sure her parents hoped the kind of sweet we were on each other would fade, but it didn't." He blew out a breath. "We were each other's first everything. We thought we'd be each other's *only* everything, too, and when we were sixteen we planned out our whole life."

"I planned out my whole life when I was sixteen too," Matilda offered. "It involved pop superstardom. Tragically, only the dogs like it when I sing."

"We were very practical," Tennessee said, and she couldn't quite decipher his tone then. Was it self-deprecating? Or something laced a bit more with the kind of grief she supposed everyone had, at some point, about the things they'd imagined they'd do when they couldn't really imagine what shape their lives might take? "I would start working in the store full-time at graduation. She would leave to get a degree, then come back so we could start building our family. We figured we'd be an unstoppable team. I started fixing up the house on the property that had been falling down my whole life for us because I had no doubt, ever, that we would do exactly what we promised each other we would do."

He shook his head and looked away. And because he was quiet for a moment, she took the opportunity to breathe in the fact that he was really *here.* Sitting on her couch, in her house, where she'd imagined him sitting a million times or more.

Though she'd never really believed a dream like that would come true. And now that he was not only here, but opening up about his life… She hadn't bothered to dream about something like that. Her imagination only went so far. This was impossible.

But he was still here.

"Long distance is hard," Tennessee told her. "We thought we could handle it, because it wasn't as if we'd ever even really lived in the same town. But it was harder than that. And not because we didn't trust each other, but because our lives became so different." He was staring straight ahead, his gaze on the fire, but Matilda suspected that he was somewhere else entirely. Somewhere back in time. "And the longer it went on, it became obvious that while her world was getting bigger and bigger with possibilities that had never occurred to us, mine was staying the same."

"I think it makes sense that your head can get turned when you live somewhere else," Matilda said quietly. "When your world changes, you change with it. That's only natural."

"Oh, her head didn't get turned," Tennessee said with a short laugh. "Mine did. If I'd listened to her, she'd never been happier, because she knew where we were heading. The plan was the plan and we were executing it exactly the way we'd dreamed up when we were sixteen. If I'd listened to her, we would probably be married now."

Matilda studied his face, and that frown he wore. "And that would be a bad thing?"

"I went to visit her on her campus in Billings," Tennessee said after a moment. "It was supposed to be a surprise, because she'd had a tough run of classes and I hadn't been able to get away. I knew her schedule, so it was easy to find her. I just waited outside for her class to let out." He shook his head. "But then when she came outside, I couldn't do it. It was like I could suddenly see it all much too clearly."

"Was she with someone else?" Matilda asked, quietly. Though inside, she was already feeling indignant on his behalf.

Tennessee let out that small laugh. "Of course she wasn't with someone else. Kacey wasn't like that. She was with her friends. And she was… light and happy and carefree. She looked like the girl she'd been in high school, the one I'd fallen in love with. And I couldn't pretend to myself any longer that she was still that girl with me."

Matilda was riveted. "I don't know what that means."

"Looking back, I can see that no matter how much I might have loved her, the important thing to me was that I made sure I was nothing like my father." Tennessee ran a hand over his face. "It's not surprising that I found someone young, held on tight, and thought that if I could do everything right, get it all locked down, I could prove that I was different. Because deep down, I was desperate to be different."

"You are different," Matilda said at once.

But Tennessee shook his head at that. "Standing there that day on her campus, when she had no idea I was anywhere around, I could see what I was doing was pulling her down with me. Chaining her somewhere that maybe she didn't belong. Because she loved me. She would never disappoint me. Even if the plans she and I made at sixteen didn't suit her anymore."

He swallowed, like it still hurt him, or maybe it was just as he was so busy looking at the past that it felt like the present again. Either way, he kept going. "I could have broken up with her on the spot and set her free immediately. I should have. But I didn't. I didn't even tell her that I was there. I went back home and I sat on it." His mouth hardened. "And that was how I figured out that given the opportunity, I was exactly like my dad. Selfish. Deeply self-centered. Perfectly willing to hurt someone else if it made me feel better. I'll tell you something, Matilda. I didn't like myself much after that."

"I think you're being unfair." Matilda studied him. "I'm pretty sure that selfish, self-centered people like themselves just fine when they act the way they do. Once again, you're nothing like him."

But he clearly didn't want to hear that. "The next time she came home, I did what had to be done. It was messy, because we'd been together so long at that point. We grew up together."

He let out a small sigh. "Needless to say, she didn't exactly see things my way. And I'll admit that we went back and forth on that. For years. Because deep down, I think we both liked the dream. The plan. The idea that two kids could get sweet on each other the first day of middle school, and make it work. Maybe they can, but we weren't those kids."

"Where is she now?" Matilda asked, already going through every person she'd ever known in Crawford County and wondering if there was a Kacey in there somewhere.

"Last I heard she was a teacher in Omaha," Tennessee said, and smiled fondly, like he was proud of her all these years later. That just made Matilda like him more. "Her mom told me that she met a nice man who thought she hung the stars and wanted to give her the world. I told her I was happy to hear it, and I meant it. They've got three kids now. She still sends my mother a Christmas card."

"Do you regret what you did?" Matilda asked. "Breaking up with her like that?"

"Not at all." He shook his head decisively. "What I regret is not cutting it off cleaner. It lingered a little too long throughout our twenties and I don't think it did either one of us any favors. Nostalgia can be a bitch like that."

He didn't say anything after that, not for some time. The fire crackled and popped. The wind slapped against the side of the cottage. Fran, Matilda's old bulldog, snored in her corner. Montgomery, the ancient dachshund, chased badgers in his sleep, his white-tipped paws scrabbling in the air as he lay on his back.

"That's the funny thing about these mysteries that folks think need solving," Tennessee said after a while. "Most of the time, they're not mysteries. They're not even secrets. Just not anybody else's business. But I'm glad to know that people are still sitting around talking about my broken heart." His blue gaze lifted to hers, and held. "That was the trouble, Matilda. It wasn't my heart that broke. And in the end, only my telling her that got her to let go. I should have told her the truth a whole lot sooner and saved her from all that mess."

"So then you became the unofficial mayor of Cowboy Point instead," Matilda said, instead of sharing her thoughts about *mess* and broken hearts and taking things on that maybe weren't his to carry. She didn't think he'd hear it. "With all of the rights and honors that conveys."

"I think we both know that the only thing it means is that people somehow think I'm a bigger busybody than they are," Tennessee said with a laugh. "Which I think we also know isn't true at all."

"I thought it had more to do with your stringent sense of responsibility for everything you touch, whether that's your family or the town," Matilda said. And thought, *or your ex-girlfriend, who you're taking responsibility for years later when she's clearly moved on.* "The very model of an upstanding citizen."

"When I decided that I couldn't solve my childhood by having a better marriage and family life than my father had," Tennessee said ruefully, "which is funny now that I know how catastrophically bad he was at those things, I figured I would lean into the things I could do something about. Cowboy Point is a unique community. I know there are always people agitating to separate from Marietta, but the truth is, we benefit from being under the Marietta umbrella. Developing our own character inside of the protection of that umbrella makes sense. It's happening more and more. Dr. Ramona opened her clinic here, not down in Marietta. We have more artists and farmers than we need at the market every summer. We're becoming such a tourist destination that we have our own mention on that up-itself website for the Resort at Ransom Ridge out in the hills, and they generally call in private helicopters to take their guests to Jackson Hole. There's even a farm-to-table restaurant, almost certain to be fancy in that Bozeman style, coming in on the main road. Classing up the valley, one step at a time."

"I've heard," Matilda said. She tilted her head as she looked at him. "I didn't really see you as the farm-to-table, fancy dinner type."

"I like any restaurant that doesn't compete for my customers," Tennessee retorted. "And I also like when other people cook dinner for me."

"I think that people underestimate what a force of good will you really are." Matilda wasn't teasing him, not exactly. But his head moved a little bit as he studied her, and she wondered if he thought that she was.

Because neither one of them was fully themselves where other people could see, were they? They were alike that way.

She liked thinking of the ways they were similar, at any

time but especially when he was sitting in her house for no particular reason on a Wednesday night in March.

"I appreciate you noticing," was all he said, so there was no particular reason that Matilda should feel as if the air was charged all around the both of them.

But it was.

She could feel it lick all over her skin. And there was something about the way Tennessee was looking at her that made her feel as if her entire body was on fire, from the inside out.

He was so absurdly beautiful, was the thing. And the more time she spent with him, the more beautiful he became. Those blue eyes of his seemed to warm the longer she looked at him, and she'd been having extremely vivid dreams about his face, and his ever-stern mouth, and how he might taste if she leaned closer, and let herself—

She cautioned herself to slow down. To take a breath.

Because this was Tennessee Lisle. The one and only.

Matilda had always liked being spontaneous. Or really, if she was honest, it was more accurate to say that she'd always been spontaneous… like it or not. What usually happened was that she would act first, think later, and when it came to men, there was usually a mess to clean up afterward.

It was, regrettably, the one way she really was like her irresponsible, selfish mother.

But Tennessee Lisle was not a hookup. Tennessee Lisle had been a driving force in her life for years. He had just… always been there. Like a tentpole that kept her whole sky up, and she'd spent a long time convincing herself she had to find somebody like him. It was the only way to deal with the silly, giggly way she felt when she was near him. Somebody like him would do the trick, she'd been sure of it.

Except it turned out there really wasn't anyone like Tennessee Lisle.

There was only the one.

And now he was on her couch. She had been in his house, and more than once.

Matilda was aware that many people were under the impression that she was incapable of parsing social interactions. This was false. She was perfectly aware of what was going on in any given social interaction, she just didn't care.

The trouble with Tennessee was that she cared entirely too much. Aside from her family, she sometimes thought he was the only person around whose opinion mattered to her at all. She'd solicited it on a thousand different occasions. She lived for months on one of his abrupt nods, or quiet, vaguely positive replies.

The urge to simply do the sort of thing she always did and fling herself at him to see what happened was strong. Almost unbearably strong. She told herself to take a breath, count to ten, get a grip.

Because she had the very strong and overwhelming feeling that if she threw herself at Tennessee, there would be no pretending it didn't happen. It would change things between them forever, no matter how he reacted.

Was she prepared for that?

"Are you going to tell me your deepest darkest secrets in return?" he asked her, and his voice was as low, and as dark, as his blue gaze was white-hot. "Like, for example, what made you decide to become the Pied Piper of Cowboy Point?"

"The Pied Piper," she echoed, and laughed, even though she wasn't sure that she could take a full breath. She was wound too tight. Her skin felt too flushed. And there was that deep, Tennessee-shaped longing twisting tighter and tighter down the center of her.

And this time, because it was him, she was very conscious of what she was doing. This time, she acknowledged that if there was a mess, it would linger there between them, possibly forever. Even if she chose to ignore it the way she ignored so many things she didn't want to think about, he would remember.

Then again, this was Tennessee Lisle. All he would do was scowl. No one would know the difference but her.

Matilda decided that she could live with that. Probably.

"Lots of people like animals. A lot also help them. But what you do is on a different level." Tennessee was looking at her so intently. "I think you know that."

"I like to think of myself as a Pied Piper," Matilda said, and she could tell that part of the giddiness inside her just then was because he was actually *asking her.* Not making up stories about her without bothering to speak to her, the way most people did. It was part of why she didn't bother with *most people.* "The truth is, I was raised by wolves. Jack took on a role he shouldn't have had to and he did his best. I was grateful for him, don't get me wrong, but what I learned from watching my parents behave badly, and then my mother make it even worse after my father died, was I prefer actual wolves to grown adults acting like wolves. Animals are better than people a lot of the time. They don't lie. They don't make promises they can't keep. They are who and what they are, every moment of the day, the end."

"And you admire that?" He was watching her, so closely. She could feel it on the inside of her skin. "That makes sense. You don't seem to care too much about rules. Responsibilities."

"Just because my responsibilities aren't broadcast all over the state of Montana for others to behold, doesn't mean they don't exist." But she smiled at him while she said that.

And the more she smiled at him, the more she could see that heat in his eyes grow. And better yet, the more he smiled back.

Matilda decided that she'd counted long enough. There was a high probability that the overly responsible Tennessee, forever concerned about honor and duty and all the rest of that nonsense that consumed him, would never make a move. So if she waited for him, she would never know.

It was one thing to not know when she'd been sure that the thing she felt about him was only in her head.

But this was different. He wasn't in her head tonight, he was in her house.

So she shifted where she sat, and slid herself over his lap, so she was straddling him.

No matter what happened next, she thought it was worth it already for that look of shock on his beautiful face, and the way his mouth opened slightly.

And that white-hot blaze of heat in his blue eyes that scorched her straight through.

His hands went to grip her hips, and she liked that.

She also knew a whole lot more things about him, immediately, simply because she'd climbed up on him like this. Because now she knew how he *felt*. His rock-hard thighs beneath hers. His hard, sculpted arms and the big, strong hands on her hips. He smelled even better up close, and she'd already thought he smelled delicious. And she could feel the heat he gave off, like he was his own furnace.

It made her hot in return, like her body wanted to match.

He blew out a breath, a sound that wasn't quite a word.

But that wasn't him ordering her to get off him.

Matilda indulged herself instead. She shifted closer, pressing herself against him, and that felt even better. Especially when she could feel the hardest part of him between them—very evidently as enthusiastic as she felt.

And that was like a lightning bolt.

So, still smiling so wide she was surprised it didn't hurt, Matilda closed the remaining distance between them, slid her arms around his neck, and kissed him.

At long last.

Chapter Eight

FOR A MOMENT, Tennessee thought his heart might explode inside his chest.

Matilda's mouth was sliding over his, and then she licked her way between his lips, and he no longer cared at all if his heart did explode. Because if he died right now, he thought he would count himself perfectly happy.

He was a big man and tiny, delicate women had never done it for him. Matilda wasn't breakable. He could feel the muscles in her thighs, the strength in her arms. She was built tough and so damned pretty and she tasted like heaven.

Perfect, in other words, because he wasn't the least bit afraid that he might hurt her.

Not that he *wanted* to hurt her, but when he sank his hands into that cloud of strawberry-blonde hair—at last—and angled her head so he could find his way deeper into this kiss, he liked very much not second-guessing himself that he might be too rough.

Then he knew beyond any shadow of a doubt that he wasn't when she moved against him, rocking herself on his lap in a way that was clearly designed to drive them both wild.

It worked, too.

It worked like a charm. After all, he'd called her the Pied Piper, and it fit—she seemed to know exactly how to use that magic on him.

Because the taste of her was almost too much to bear. She tasted like sugar. Her mouth was hot, and fit his perfectly. The way she kissed him seemed hotwired to something deep inside of him, like he'd been waiting his whole life for her to flip this exact switch.

He moved, tipping her over so he could stretch them both out on the couch, and that was even better.

The kiss deepened, then got wilder. Much wilder. He found his hands moving of their own accord, finding their way beneath her clothes so he could touch her skin. He felt her hands on him, tracing fire along his spine, her fingers digging into him as she kissed him in a way that made him think that maybe he'd never been kissed before.

She felt flushed, her lips were soft and sweet, and he wanted to put his mouth on every last part of her.

He kissed her again and again, and they rolled over once more, and then she was laughing and he was surprised to find that he was laughing too as they tumbled their way onto the floor.

But she didn't stop kissing him. And he couldn't stop kissing her.

He wasn't sure he would have stopped—ever—if one of her dogs hadn't come over then and insinuated his great, big, shaggy head between them.

Matilda laughed as she fended the big shepherd off. She

sat up and rubbed the dog on his furry face. "Silly boy," she crooned at him. "So protective."

She rolled up to her feet in a smooth way that told Tennessee more things about her and that mouthwatering body of hers. Then she let out a sharp whistle that had all the dogs following her as she led them into the kitchen. He heard a lot of dog toenails scrabbling on the floor and a few barks, and when she came back out she closed the door to the kitchen behind her so they couldn't follow.

Then she stood there by the door, her gray-blue gaze on him like she was waiting for him to object. To stand up and head for the door. To cut this off right now, before it got more complicated.

It was like she'd read his mind.

Because this was not the kind of thing Tennessee did.

Ever.

It felt almost painful, the clarity he had suddenly. It was like he could page back to every single interaction he'd had with this woman, going back years. Like they were all laid out before him, finally impossible to ignore.

In every single one of them, he'd worked hard to pretend he couldn't see her. To pretend his body didn't respond to her. To pretend, over and over, that she was just a neighbor. The younger sister of an old friend. Nothing more, nothing less.

In this moment, here in her house with the taste of her in his mouth, he was doing none of that work. And he could see how much effort he'd put into it over the years. How he'd been lying to himself, on some level, for at least the last decade.

Which would track. Since that was right around the time Kacey had left for the last time. She'd finally let him go and she'd been married within two years to a guy who looked at her like he'd won the lottery. Tennessee had expected to grieve that. To pat himself on the back for being some kind of martyr—but that had never happened. He hadn't grieved Kacey at all, or not as much as he'd grieved that same idea of them at sixteen that they'd both held onto for much too long.

That had been telling.

Tonight, though, he was pretty sure that it was around that time that he'd started noticing Matilda. And not in the way that anyone else noticed Matilda. They all saw the eclectic clothes, the often messy hair, the truckful of animals.

But Tennessee, if he let himself, had a perfect memory of Matilda Stark at about twenty-two.

It had been summer. All of that golden light extending so late into the evenings made everybody giddy, and a little bit drunk on it all. He couldn't remember what he'd been doing to find himself out by the river that stretched across their little valley, cutting across the main road, and down past the Coppermine, continuing along until it reached the church tucked in the foothills on the other side. In the summer, folks waded and floated about in the water, tubed across the valley floor, and swam in the swimming hole.

That particular evening must have been hot for Tennessee to have wandered down to the swimming hole. He couldn't remember. What he could recall, perfectly, was Matilda.

He hadn't been prepared to be standing there as she came up out of the water. She'd been slicked all over, wet and glistening in the evening light. Her hair had been dark from the water but still curly as it flowed down past her shoulders, but what he'd really been focused on was the bolt of heat that went through him at the wholly unexpected sight of Matilda Stark in a bikini.

It hadn't even been a particularly revealing bikini. He supposed that it would be called a two-piece to distinguish it from the more deliberately sexy versions. Hers had been very *her*. It had been more like a sports bra of a top and little shorts.

Tennessee shouldn't have cared. He shouldn't have noticed.

But he had never seen that much of Matilda's body. She was dusted in freckles, and clearly spent time outside in not much more than she was wearing that night, since she was tan all over. She'd had water sandals on her feet, the way everyone did getting in and out of the river, and she'd appeared to have absolutely no awareness that Tennessee had just about swallowed his own tongue at the sight of her.

At all of that soft, golden flesh. He'd had an urge at the time that had struck him as borderline insane. He'd wanted to go over to her, kneel down in front of her, and press his face to the swell of her belly. He'd wanted to lose himself in all that slick gold.

He had the same urge now. But unlike then, he wasn't pretending to himself that he wasn't wildly attracted to her.

And he had no intention of leaving.

Matilda moved toward him and took his hands in hers. Then she tipped her head back to look up at him, and he got the feeling she liked how much taller he was than her as much as he did.

"I have an idea," she said. He could see all that heat in her gaze, and all over her face. He could feel it answer in him. "What if you let me take you upstairs, lay you down, and have my way with you? You won't have to be responsible for anything."

"If you have your way with me, that would mean I'm also having my way with you," he heard himself reply, as if someone else had taken over his body. "Seems to me I'd have some responsibilities there."

Her smile was better than the best summer, he thought. It seemed to crack him wide open.

And the trouble was, Tennessee knew himself.

He knew himself too well, so when she only shrugged and tugged him after her as she headed for the stairs and then led him up them, he knew better.

Because he wasn't a casual guy. When he felt something, it felt like forever.

And Matilda was all light and air, dancing about as a whim took her. He had never believed that she was quite as fluttery as she pretended she was sometimes, just as he'd never found her to be anything like her mother.

But Matilda didn't settle. Matilda's passions in life were temporary. Oh yes, she loved animals, but what she loved was rescuing them and then rehoming them and then moving on to rescue others.

Meanwhile, Tennessee had never met a task he couldn't make a daily chore or any kind of commitment he couldn't turn into a lifetime of obsessive dedication.

The one girlfriend he'd had he had decided he wanted to marry before he really understood what that meant.

He was all about settling down, hard. Matilda was all about setting herself free.

There was no possible way that this could work out between them, and he knew that. He knew it even as she took him upstairs and led him down the hall to the room at the end. He knew it and he did nothing to stop it.

Hell, he participated.

She pulled him into the bedroom with her and he was not at all surprised to find that it was a riot of color. The bed was covered in brightly hued pillows and a patchwork sort of quilt in almost too many vivid shades to name. She had painted the walls a dark turquoise and almost every piece of furniture in it was a different, clashing color—except altogether, it felt happy. Joyful. And very much like Matilda.

It was also not remotely messy, which he couldn't help thinking was an essential truth about this woman. Something she kept hidden, like the outbuilding that everyone assumed she kept in some kind of wild state when he'd seen for himself the care she had to put into it to keep it clean. Everyone assumed that everything she touched was as disheveled as she sometimes was, he hadn't seen that here in the house.

Clutter wasn't the same thing as dirty, and her bedroom wasn't even cluttered. It was cozy and it faced east, so when the sun felt like rising in these dark months, it would make everything shine. Matilda most of all.

That image threatened to undo him.

She pushed him back so he sat down on the bed, and he let her. Right then he would have let her do anything.

And as he watched, she continued to smile so brightly and beautifully straight at him as she began to peel off her clothes.

Surely, he would say something at any moment to put the brakes on this, to contain it or redirect it, but he didn't.

Because she was acting out the fantasy he'd had all those years ago. And as he watched, she stripped down until she was finally standing before him, gloriously naked.

Then she gazed at him, expectantly, and he felt something seem to clutch inside his chest.

Because he wanted, more than anything, to be the man she saw when she looked at him like this. He wanted, for the first time in his life, to be someone other than Tennessee Lisle. Not that he had anything against himself, but it turned out that he was tired of the persona he'd built up around his name.

He wanted to be the man he saw reflected in her gray eyes. Because he could see that she found him hot. Exciting. And maybe just a little bit dangerous.

He'd never been so hard. He'd never wanted a woman more.

She was like a fantasy come to life, and he refused to let himself ruin it. So he didn't say a word.

He only stripped off his own clothes in reply, and stood

up so he could swing her up into his arms at last.

At last, because it felt overdue. As if they'd been working toward this forever, because it felt as if they had, even while it also felt as if this had all happened so fast. It was a rush, a breathlessness, yet at the same time it felt inevitable.

Undeniable. As if there had never been any possibility that they would end up anywhere but here.

Matilda wrapped herself around him, pressing her perfect breasts to his chest. Tennessee tipped them both over, back down onto that bedspread, and then he lost track of time.

Because the only thing there was, the only thing that mattered, was Matilda.

The way their bodies fit together. Her curves against the wall of his chest. The prick of her nipples and their velvety texture against his skin.

He followed the urge he'd had so many years ago and put his mouth on her skin. He traced his way from her belly, down lower, tasting gold all the way. He kept going until he could find her sweet heat, where he settled in and demonstrated what a little bit of stern responsibility and daily discipline could do.

A few times, just to make sure he was imparting the right message.

Only when he had her bucking her hips and crying out his name for the third time did he move on. He flipped her over so he could finally admit to himself how deeply obsessed he was with that butt of hers that he was forever seeing around town and had wanted to get his hands on for what seemed like a lifetime.

He indulged himself there, too.

When she pushed against him, tipping him over so she could crawl on top of him, he let that happen. And she wasn't any easier on him.

The way she touched him made his heart seem to crack hard against his ribs. She looked filled with wonder. Like he was a gift, and everywhere she touched him he felt like fire—and she shivered like she could feel the same heat in her.

The same damn flame.

And when it got to be too much, Tennessee jackknifed up to a sitting position, but she only slid her knees up higher so they were sitting the same way they'd been down on the couch.

"I'm completely clean," she told him, with a frown, like she wanted to make sure he knew she was being serious. "I'm not saying that flippantly. I'm scrupulous about testing, whether I have any reason to be or not."

"Noted." Tennessee smoothed his hands over that wild hair of hers, all those silken red-gold waves. "I am also clean. Not because I've been scrupulously tested, but because time would tell tales if there were any to tell."

"That sounded almost poetic, Tennessee." She shifted slightly, there where she sat pressed up tight against him, and he could feel how hard and hot he was against all of her softness. Touching her heat. Close, but not quite there. "Are you telling me it's been a long time?"

"It feels like a lifetime," he said. "It's definitely been years."

"Years." She looked baffled, and it was almost unbearably

hot to witness. "Why?"

"Because I have certain preferences," he told her, his attention on the perfect shape of her ears. "And I see no point in pretending otherwise. It only leads to frustration."

"Preferences," she echoed. "How exciting. Do you—"

But Tennessee was finished talking.

He took her head between his hands and he kissed her, long and deep. Once, then again, and when he was ready he pulled back just enough.

"Shut up, Matilda," he ordered her, his mouth still touching hers. "Decide if you want to use a condom or not."

"I'm good," she whispered against his lips. "But I—"

"Why don't you let me take care of this," he suggested, and he couldn't seem to keep from smiling. "You can tell me later if you have any complaints. Okay?"

And he could feel her melt. Her whole body was a shiver. He could feel it there in that sweet heat between her legs, and that shiver kept on going.

"Okay," she whispered.

So Tennessee kissed her again, and then he reached down, set his hands beneath her butt, and lifted her up. She was already breathing hard, so all he did then was play a little bit, holding her up as he moved himself, just the very tip, through her wild, glorious heat.

Then, lifting his gaze so he could pin all that gray and blue fire with his, he lowered her down. Inch by agonizingly perfect inch, and he watched her flush. Then break out in a kind of sweat. Then open her mouth to gasp, though he did not speed up. He kept going slow.

Then slower still, to give her time to accommodate him.

And then, when he lowered her fully and he was in her deep, she tipped forward a little bit with her eyes closed tight and pressed her forehead to his.

"I think…" She breathed out, and it was shaky. "I think that if I just…"

"You're not doing anything," he told her. "Remember?"

But he moved her up just a little bit and then sank her back down hard, and she imploded.

It came on her quick, like a punch, then shook through her again and again.

And it took an iron sort of will to ride that out and to keep from falling over that cliff himself, but Tennessee was nothing if not perfectly capable of asserting his will over anything and everything.

He'd made it the project of his life, and now he understood why.

It was all worth it so he could hold himself still as Matilda sobbed against him, and only then, when she finally came back to herself—her eyes something like silver with all of that passion and pleasure—did he move her up a little bit to settle on her knees.

Then he gripped her hips and began to move.

And there was no pretending that this wasn't intimate. They were staring straight at each other. There was no hiding.

It was raw, intense, and felt so damn good that Tennessee was surprised with each stroke that he could keep going.

But he did. He was that determined. He built her back

up, one deep thrust after the next, maintaining his pace even when her breath caught again. Even when she tried to work a little bit of her own magic with those hips of hers that he thought might haunt him forever.

He maintained the same rhythm. It was drugging. It was extraordinary.

It was, he was certain, perhaps the biggest mistake he'd ever made in his life and he was loving every single second of it.

And finally, he watched a flush work its way all over her. It stained her cheeks and her neck and found its way down the front of her chest as he gripped her hard and began to move a little faster.

A little deeper.

Her nails dug deep into his shoulders. She threw her head back, her hair everywhere and her mouth open, as if this was a joy too great to bear.

He kept going, finding that place inside of her that she couldn't seem to handle—and when he rubbed himself there, stroke after stroke after stroke, she fell apart.

This time, he let himself fall with her.

And what a way to go. He felt as if he was torn apart and scattered like glass, though he was sure that every last glittering piece of him could feel every matching, gleaming shard that was her.

It seemed like a thousand years later that they were reconstituted, themselves again, and he lay with her on that bright, happy bed and held her as she lay there, passed out hard in his arms.

She snored, and it was adorable. She was hot and warm and sweet against him. And he felt as if his heart had left his body entirely.

He suspected he knew exactly where it was.

Tennessee did not intend to sleep much this night, either. And she was even sweeter than a litter of adorable puppies.

But he could already feel the shift inside of him. It had already happened—maybe it had happened all those years ago at the swimming hole and this had been a losing game ever since. Whenever it had happened, what mattered was that he could already tell that it was too late.

And that meant Tennessee was going to have to figure out how to tell her—and everyone else, and himself while he was at it, and more dangerous, *her*—that what he needed from Matilda Stark was the thing she was very unlikely to give.

Not just herself. He figured she'd be happy enough with that.

But what he wanted from her was forever.

Chapter Nine

MATILDA WAS WELL used to her spontaneous, not-even-remotely-thought-out decisions having consequences. That was the price of spontaneity. On balance, she usually felt that it was worth it.

But a consequence she had not thought to prepare herself for, and could not possibly have imagined preparing herself for, was… suddenly finding herself in some kind of *thing* with Tennessee.

Matilda couldn't allow herself to name it. She hardly dared believe it was happening, much less in a way that required *categorization*.

She expected to wake up that first morning and find him gone, but he was still there when she opened her eyes in the darkness of the wee hours. Sleeping beside her in her bed, wrapped up with her as if they'd spent many nights just like this. Right there in the bedroom where she had spent a whole lot of time making up stories about him in her head.

For years.

She could hardly be blamed for throwing herself on him and waking him up in a manner that had him calling out her name and gripping her headboard like he wanted to break it in half. And he nearly did, before he returned the favor in kind.

That had all been deeply satisfying.

It wasn't even dawn yet when he left, which in some circumstances she might have felt was him sneaking out. But this was Tennessee. He did not *sneak* anywhere.

Matilda reminded herself that he had to get down to the diner before five, just like every morning, and he certainly wouldn't want anyone to see his truck parked up here at this hour. That would start the kind of gossip that Matilda might have been used to, given her eccentricities that so many people liked to comment on, but Tennessee was different. Folks didn't whisper about his personal life too much these days. They whispered about his accomplishments, his mood, and whether or not they thought he would support new ventures in the valley.

There was no way that he would be a fan of speculation about his social life. It wasn't personal, she told herself as she stood at the window and watched his taillights as he drove away. He was used to being a little more private, that was all.

She hadn't given him her cell phone number. That had been deliberate. If she knew he had it, some part of her would be waiting to see if he used it. That was only natural.

This way she couldn't torture herself, waiting for him to call.

When the old landline rang that night, she assumed it was the usual spam callers. She liked to answer those and pretend to be a variety of different people for her own amusement, so she swiped up the old handheld—

And was not at all prepared to hear Tennessee's voice on the other end.

"Come over," he said, his voice low, and impossible, and *urgent*.

And every single thing she might possibly want to hear.

"Okay," she managed to say.

She might even have giggled. *Giggled*. A sound she was sure she had otherwise never uttered in all her life.

He hadn't told her to pull in around back, behind the General Store so her truck couldn't be seen from the street, but she did. No one needed to know where she was. No one needed to know anything about this.

Whatever this was, it was theirs alone.

When she walked onto his porch, he was already opening the front door to let her in. And they didn't make it much farther.

And it turned out that when she was in his arms, Matilda didn't really care if the whole world knew. She thought that maybe she might shout it out the windows, as a matter of fact, though she restrained herself.

They lay in front of the fire for a long while. He made her a very late dinner, or maybe it was more of a snack, and then he carried her upstairs into his bedroom and laid her on the bed there.

"This is not as monastic as I expected," Matilda said, looking around at the quiet, comfortable furnishings. The leather chair in one corner with another bookshelf and a reading lamp. The color scheme that was tame by her standards, but also wasn't neutral white, suggesting he'd painted this all himself. The overall effect was soothing and kind of brainy at once.

He just kept getting hotter.

"Why would it be monastic at all?" Tennessee asked, frowning down at her—but now when he frowned at her, he usually smiled. It was a whole different kind of exchange. She usually felt it sizzle its way through her, and now was no exception.

"You know. Your whole…" She waved a hand at him. *"Thing."*

"My thing is that I'm neat and orderly, like a fully grown adult who likes and takes care of what he owns," Tennessee said in what sounded to Matilda like repressive tones.

She grinned at him. "Of course. You in no way have control issues."

"Only people who lack control think others have too much of it," he retorted.

Matilda laughed. And when she insisted that it was her turn to mess him up until he lost a little of that control he was so proud of, he laughed right back at her. Then he crawled on top of her and had her forgetting her own damn name.

March continued to storm and stamp its way toward spring, and Matilda expected every day that this would end. But they kept going.

It had been a few weeks, maybe even a month, when Matilda stopped pretending and started asking herself if she was really in some kind of *relationship* with Tennessee.

Though she never used that word.

Not even in her own head.

But they saw each other almost every night. One of them would go to the other's house late and leave early. They both had pretty early mornings, though Tennessee's was always the earliest, so there was no need to discuss it. She would drive home from work, feeling shivery—and not in the way she normally did when going over Copper Mountain in the winter.

In fact, she was far more impatient than normal, when she knew how careful she had to be in her little truck.

Driving through town to get to her cottage was torturous. She just wanted to go to Tennessee, but she couldn't. Her life involved a great many animals, by choice, and there was no getting around that. She didn't really *want* to get around it, though sometimes she had to remind herself of that in these heady, wild Tennessee days.

She went home and spent time with her pets. She cared for all her rescues. And sometimes, she had to deal with her own family, too.

Those nights were the hardest, because family dinners almost always meant she'd be sleeping alone. Matilda loved her family, and she loved the dinners that Jack liked to have up in his caretaker's cottage at the Lodge. But she was only really happy again when Tennessee was coming to her front door the next night, or when she slipped down the hill to see him.

She wasn't sleeping much, but Matilda thought it was worth it. After all, she didn't expect this little fever of theirs to last.

They'd been sneaking around for a full month and change when Tennessee told her that, unbeknownst to her, he'd been working on her rescue idea all along. When she would have bet money on him never mentioning her name in public, in case someone read the truth on him.

"Of course," she said, trying to look serious and not... shocked. "The rescue. The reason we got together in the first place."

They were in his house that night. She was wearing one of his T-shirts, and had broken him enough that he brought her food to eat in his bedroom. Matilda didn't need him to tell her that this was not something he normally permitted himself. She could tell.

He had made her a rich, hearty stew to ward off the latest snowstorm. It had simmered all day, he'd told her when she'd arrived and had breathed in all that deliciousness in the air. And now he served it with a bit of crusty, yeasty bread that she was fairly certain he'd baked himself. When she'd complimented him, he had scowled at her—without a smile—and had told her that if he couldn't provide her a decent meal, then he might as well close the diner and leave town. For good.

She had no idea that men—or rather, Tennessee, the most perfect of men—could be so *dramatic*. Matilda knew better than to say that to him, but privately, she was delighted. She loved all these clues that really, they were the same.

"I didn't forget about your rescue," he told her, and here in private, he touched her all the time. Like it hurt him to live through all the hours they were apart during the day and couldn't touch her like this. She was familiar with that quiet little agony. Tennessee leaned over to kiss her on the nose. "I've been talking to old Mrs. Bonney. You know who she is."

"Of course," Matilda said at once. "Mrs. Bonney was a schoolteacher here for a long time. Back when there was only one teacher in a one-room schoolhouse, if I'm remembering right. I'm pretty sure she knew my grandparents. She might even have taught my father."

"More than likely." Tennessee smiled. "She's an institution. She also owns that strip of land right there at the bottom of the hill below the Lodge. More important for animal rescue purposes, she also owns that big, old barn that all the tourists take pictures of."

Matilda stopped shoveling the stew he'd made into her mouth, which was hard, because it was outrageously good. She fancied herself something of an artisan soup maker in cold weather, but she had nothing on Tennessee.

Yet she wasn't sure she could allow herself to believe what he was telling her. Or what she *thought* he was telling her.

Slow down, she told herself. *You've made up enough stories about this man in your life as it is.*

"She wants to sit down with you and her lawyer down in Marietta," Tennessee told her, correctly interpreting her silence. "Because one thing everyone might not know about Mrs. Bonney is that she's a cat lady. I think she has something like ten cats in that house with her right now and I've never known her to say no to a kitten."

"She sounds like my kind of lady," Matilda said.

"She knows who you are," Tennessee told her. "She said she would never consider trusting an animal's life to anyone except *that girl in the red truck* and if she can help you make that dream of a rescue come true, she will." He grinned at the look on her face, and Matilda knew it had to be something like dumbstruck. "Before you get too sappy on me, I think it made her feel good to have somewhere to leave not only some of her property, but all of those cats."

"She can depend on me to take care of her babies like they are my own," Matilda vowed fervently, cats unseen.

Something she repeated in person to Mrs. Bonney herself when they got together the next week. She sat in the old woman's sweet little house, filled with the kind of clutter that Matilda was very careful never to allow hers to become—but hey, life was long—with a big, fat calico cat purring happily in her lap.

"I always wanted to be a rescuer sort myself," Mrs. Bonney said as they sipped tea and ate sugar cookies from a tin that tasted like butter. "But I only end up making pets of them, I'm afraid."

"In the end, that's the goal, isn't it?" Matilda asked. "We want them to have families. Seems like yours are perfectly happy right here with you, where they belong."

Mrs. Bonney gazed at her for a long moment. "They all said I went a bit odd after my Peter died. But between you and me, though I was certainly fond of him, he had a hard limit on cats." She didn't shift her gaze from Matilda's, and Matilda couldn't repress the urge to sit up taller in her seat.

"My advice to you, if I may, is to never, ever accept cat limitations. Not only does that lead to fewer cats, it tends to be emblematic of other issues." She nodded, with a sniff. "The less said about that, the better."

"Mrs. Bonney," Matilda said in the same intense way, "I have not accepted a cat, dog, or small mammal limitation yet."

The old woman smiled, her cheeks creasing. "I knew I liked you."

And that was how Pied Piper Rescue, Matilda's dream come true, started in the rundown old Bonney barn that was going to need a whole lot of TLC to get going. Matilda was no stranger to the TLC side of things. She'd transformed the outbuilding behind the cottage all by herself.

What mattered was that it was real. And it was happening.

Even if Matilda couldn't really explain *why* it was happening to all the interested parties who she had to tell about the new venture. Like her sister and brother and all of her extremely nosy cousins.

"So Tennessee Lisle just took it upon himself to suddenly become deeply interested in animal welfare, and hunt down this old woman with this barn, and convince her to do this?" Rosie asked one morning, having come to the barn while Matilda was busy working there on her day off.

"As you know, Rosie," Matilda said airily, "Tennessee takes the welfare of the town very seriously. Why not the animals as well?"

"Yeah, right," Rosie said, studying Matilda suspiciously.

Especially when Matilda aimed her vaguest smile her way. "That sounds like him."

Her brother Jack was even more dubious.

"Did you bribe him or something?" he asked gruffly.

"Jack," Matilda said impatiently. "If you don't want to help me clear out this barn, I don't really know why you're here. I thought you were the renovation king."

"I don't understand why this is happening," her cousin Wyatt chimed in, gruffly.

"Who just swoops in and makes all this happen out of the goodness of his heart?" Logan, another cousin, demanded.

"Not Tennessee Lisle," her other male cousin answered shortly.

She had corralled them all here on a Sunday afternoon because they were brawny and covered in muscles and she did not want to lug all the debris inside the barn out herself.

"I have always wanted to open a rescue," she told them all, folding her arms and glaring each one of them in turn, just in case they were under the impression that she really was as ditzy as her mother. When they should know better. "I discussed this lifelong dream of mine with Tennessee, who as you may know, having grown up here, has his fingers in everything. That means he knows exactly who, for example, has an old barn sitting around with nothing to do. What is difficult to comprehend about this?"

"And he's helping you renovate it too?" Wyatt asked, sounding darkly dubious. Like Tennessee's help was nefarious, somehow.

"He might, yes," Matilda said, glaring at him. "Because—and again, I don't know if any of you are aware of this in between your questionable trips down into Marietta to hang out at the Wolf Den and make fools of yourselves—but *some people* actually care about Cowboy Point. And are invested in its growth. And community-based organizations like animal rescues, just to pull something out of a hat, are good for communities. It pulls people together. It makes them feel like they all belong to a place that cares about them and the things they care about in return. I know none of this is meaningful to you three since you all run wild and are literally known for nothing but your escapades, but *other people, grown people*—"

"We get it," muttered Noah.

"My God," Logan agreed. "I'll renovate the damn barn myself just to make you shut up."

"Your assistance is appreciated and accepted," Matilda shot back.

And because she made sure to make her family as miserable as possible, they got the barn cleared out pretty fast, too.

It was when Sara Jane showed up that things got trickier. Because she came with her crew of best friends in tow. Esther Wayne, whose true crime podcast was the only thing better than coffee in the mornings when Matilda was inching her way down the slick side of Copper Mountain on her way to work. Juliet Cross, one of the elementary school teachers—and the one Mrs. Bonney had mentioned by name, admiringly. And Kitty Bennett, the culinary genius behind the best pizza around.

"Did I see Tennessee Lisle in here the other day?" Esther asked, which meant that she had absolutely seen Tennessee right here, probably seventeen times, before she asked.

"He helped put this all together," Matilda said. It was another Sunday, and the girls had come by to see the place before Matilda started transporting the animals she still had in the outbuilding up at the cottage. "He likes to come by from time to time and see how it's going. Even helped put together the kennels and the runs."

This was all true. It was equally true that out here in rural Montana, things that took months for city folks happened fast. Especially at this time of year, when the snowmelt wasn't happening fast enough and every man with a toolbox was only too happy to lend a hand to a project that would get him outside.

It was also true that she and Tennessee had celebrated all of these truths and accomplishments, naked.

Though not here.

"I've never known Tennessee to be at all helpful," Sara Jane said, studying Matilda much too closely for her liking.

But Matilda gave her nothing, even if she wanted to bristle in Tennessee's defense. She made herself laugh instead.

"Are we talking about the same Tennessee?" she asked. "Grumpy, I grant you, but since when is he unhelpful? Remember the Farm & Craft Market last summer? Sure, he refuses to put up a booth for the store or the diner, but that Saturday when it was so hot, who was out there handing out drinks?"

Kitty nodded. "That is true. He's like his own sneaky,

kind of off-putting chamber of commerce."

Sara Jane did not look convinced. Esther looked *intrigued*, which did not bode well.

Still, Matilda delighted in telling Tennessee what Kitty had said later that same night. When he was deep inside of her, slamming into her from behind.

"Obviously not off-putting enough," he growled, gripping her hips in that hard, masterful way of his that made her nearly shiver herself over a cliff just remembering, later.

Rosie rustled up her husband and brothers-in-law to help Matilda get the animals down the hill one afternoon, and they did that so quickly that she was surprised. She'd been certain it would take a lot longer. Multiple days, endless trips. But the Careys handled it in an hour or two, like it was nothing.

"We're ranchers," Ryder told her with a grin. "It's literally in our blood to move animals from one space to another space, repeat forever."

"Some of us are good ranchers," the oldest Carey brother, Harlan, said with a laugh. "So if there's maybe a little more art to it than that, Ryder wouldn't know. He's still got the rodeo in his head."

The Carey brothers, who always spent time together and seemed to enjoy each other's company even with all the teasing, had always been a kind of mystery to Matilda. Her brother Jack was solitary and dark, and she thought that he took pleasure in that. Her cousins were, always, wild. She and her sister and Sara Jane had never really fit the mold around here. Rosie had gone and gotten pregnant and hadn't intended to tell anyone who the father was. Matilda was, well. She was herself. And Sara Jane hid it a little better, but she was just as strange. She just dressed it up behind books at the library. The Starks had always been a little edgier.

The Careys were wholesome. *Sweet.* Though Rosie had cackled when Matilda had advanced that theory. There was certainly no denying that they were also remarkably good-looking. Not just good-looking, but *hot*.

Now they were also all married. They'd gone from a whole lot of bachelors who made the women around town act like fools to a whole lot of weddings and babies in record time. Matilda couldn't imagine that happening in her family. Nobody liked the Starks that much.

"I've never known a Lisle to put himself out unless there's something in it for him," Boone Carey said as they got the last of the dogs situated in the new kennel area.

"That's because it's never happened in the history of Lisles," the youngest Carey brother, Knox, chimed in.

Wilder Carey, Ryder's twin and the only member of the family who was actually married to a Lisle, sighed mightily. "With enough training, a Lisle can be a perfectly decent human being," he said.

Matilda stared straight at him. "I am absolutely telling your wife that you said that. And you know she'll believe me. I'm not a liar."

All the Careys laughed at that, even while Wilder shrugged it off—though Matilda was pretty sure there was healthy fear in his eyes. The sign of a good marriage, in her opinion.

Still, after they left her with promises that they'd be happy to help at a moment's notice again, if she needed it—"because anything that makes Rosie happy makes me happy," Ryder drawled, "and I'm happier still to make my brothers help me do that"—Matilda found herself fuming a little bit.

Truth was, she didn't really like people casting aspersions on Tennessee. Or his family in general. She wanted to defend him. She had to bite her own tongue to keep herself from defending him. The only reason she didn't was because she thought it would call too much attention to the very thing that too many people were clearly already suspicious about.

But the reality was that she hated listening to anyone talk smack about Tennessee, or his family, or anything connected to him in any way.

She felt it simmering inside of her, like it wanted to come out. Like it would, if she let it. When she knew better than to allow that to happen. It would ruin everything.

If Tennessee didn't want this to be a secret, it wouldn't be. Matilda was determined to respect that.

Then she stood there, in the middle of this new rescue space that had come together so quickly, and almost too easily, and she should have been thinking about absolutely nothing but that. She should have been beside herself, tending to all these animals and figuring out how she'd make sure that they were just as comfortable here as they'd been before.

The husky, of course, was already keeping watch, like

this had been his plan from the start.

But Matilda realized something then. Something stunning. For the first time in her life, she was passionately invested in something other than animals.

And that kind of took the breath right out of her.

She had to sit with it for a long time.

So long that Tennessee came to find her later that afternoon, still standing there feeling sucker punched in the rescue, because she hadn't answered her phone.

He walked in, big and tall and even more beautiful now that she knew him so much more intimately than she had before. He gave her a quizzical look as he drew near, and put his hand on her upper arm like he needed to touch her.

She'd been in love with him for so long now. But there was loving him before that night, and there was loving him after. The fantasy versus the reality.

Reality was so much better, it was almost funny. And Matilda was positive that this form of loving him was going to stick with her forever. Deep in her bones, she understood that he was a part of her now.

That was probably not something he was going to want to hear. She understood that. She couldn't blame him. He was who he was. So was she. The smart move would be to keep her mouth shut and continue to enjoy this thing they had. It had been more than six weeks now. Summer was coming. Everything was better in the summer.

Yet as much as it scared her, and as much as the idea of not being cool at all and probably ruining everything terrified her, she didn't think that she could keep this inside any longer.

Because she wanted to defend him. Maybe she needed to, because she wanted to make it clear to everyone that she was not a safe space for any Tennessee slander or insinuations of any kind. Or she had to stop this, because it was going to come out of its own accord and then everyone would know.

That would be the worst possible outcome. She was certain of that.

"What are you doing?" he asked. "I have food for you in the house if you're coming by later, but it's Wednesday, so—"

"I love you," Matilda blurted out. "I've been in love with you for so long that I forgot you didn't know, and then I couldn't tell you, because I knew that if you did know…" She shook her head, her heart like a sledgehammer inside her chest and oh, she was sure she could feel the damage. "I love you so much, Tennessee. And I couldn't not tell you any longer. It was beginning to feel like a lie. So."

He stood there and stared back at her, and she couldn't read the look on his face.

That hurt, because she'd been able to read him for years now. And she knew him better now, so she should have been able to read him even more closely. The fact that she couldn't…

And she understood, then, that she could not bear to watch him recoil.

She would not survive it.

"I love you," she said again, because it was true and also to forestall anything he might have been about to say.

Because she should have thought this through, but like all things Matilda, she'd just jumped right in. Now she was paying for that. And would keep paying for that. "You don't have to say anything. I just need you to know that."

And then she ran out of the rescue barn, climbed into her truck, and drove away before he could break her heart any more than she already had, all by herself.

Chapter Ten

Every instinct Tennessee had was to run after her, possibly tackle her to the ground, and explain to her what he'd known since pretty much the beginning.

That *of course* this was forever, and why did she think he was so sure about that?

But he didn't.

He stayed where he was. He listened to her truck drive away a little too recklessly, as far as he was concerned, but he knew she'd only laugh at him if he said something like that. And as he stood there in the airy barn that she'd transformed—using her vision of what she wanted and a whole lot of help—it was as if all the rescue dogs understood the gravity of the situation, because they quieted down like they were listening too.

"It's okay," Tennessee told them.

He nodded toward the one he considered the leader of the rescue pack, because he was standing apart from the rest of them like he had a higher calling. Tennessee had learned that he was a mix of husky, obviously, and maybe some shepherd or possibly wolf. What Tennessee knew was that he and this dog had the same eyes.

"I've got this," Tennessee assured him, and after nearly two months in Matilda's world, it didn't feel the slightest bit strange to him that he was having a conversation with this dog. Or even that he considered it a *conversation* in the first place.

The dog, who Tennessee was pretty sure would be coming home with him one of these nights, whined his agreement. Then went back to his watch.

A man after his own heart, to Tennessee's mind.

Matilda had nailed Tennessee's issue with pets accurately, which shouldn't have surprised him. She was pretty talented at hitting those bullseyes. He wouldn't have thought anyone remembered the dog he'd had when he was a kid, but naturally she did.

She'd also understood that losing Angus really had ripped Tennessee's heart out. Angus had been the only thing that was his. The only creature who might have looked to him, but also looked out for him. He'd been sixteen when the puppy he'd picked out from a litter outside the market down in Marietta looked at him for the last time, pressed his grizzled, white muzzle into Tennessee's hand, and blew out his last breath.

Maybe it wasn't such a big shock that the very next thing Tennessee had done was rustle up some permanence. He and Kacey had made their plans. He'd decided that was what he needed to focus on, not pets.

And Matilda had divined this somehow, because she was magic like that.

She was magical, full stop.

He wasn't sure why no one seemed to know that but him. Including her.

Tennessee walked outside and took a deep breath of the evening air. March was still delivering the cold and wet, with a snowstorm for good measure. He thought maybe a person had to be a Montana native to catch the faintest hint of spring in all that winter, but it was there. Faint, but there.

It always smelled like hope.

Tonight was a Wednesday and it was much lighter at nearly 6 PM than it had been some six weeks ago now, when he'd joined the LPL Club for its inaugural meeting. And had then found Matilda on his doorstep when he'd come home. For the second night in a row.

If it wasn't a Wednesday night, he thought he probably would have chased her back to her cottage right now. Maybe even beaten her up the hill, given the mood he was in.

But even as he thought that, he decided he was happy that he had this commitment that he, by God, wouldn't be the first to break.

Because he already knew what would happen if he followed her back home. It would be what always happened. The chemistry between them only seemed to get more intense, and it took over sometimes. Maybe too much, because it didn't take an expert on relationships to figure out that there were some issues in need of exploring here. Or why would a woman who spent all of her free time with a man who quite clearly doted on her tell him she loved him and then take off running?

He was going to have to think about that.

And he knew he wouldn't get much thinking done if he chased her down now.

Still, he stood outside for a while, letting the cold settle in on him while he frowned up the hill toward the Lodge. He waited until he saw the lights go on in her cottage.

Not that seeing those lights made it any easier to get in his truck and drive back down the length of the main drag to his house so he could park it outside Mountain Mama's. Dutifully.

But he did it.

Inside, it was the usual happy atmosphere with some old-school folk music playing from the speakers and tables full of chattering neighbors. That hint of spring was making everyone excited, he figured. But he stopped at every table he passed to say hello.

Not because he thought he was the mayor. But because he knew folks, or he'd seen them around town, or he'd heard something about them through the old-timer grapevine that sat at his counter every morning and functioned like a chorus of town criers.

If Tennessee ever had the urge to become one of the town gossips, he would put the rest of them out of a job in a hurry, because he knew everything.

But part of the reason people liked to tell him things was because he didn't pass them on. Because they thought he was a vault. Only tonight did he consider the fact that this line of thinking wasn't necessarily because they thought he was so circumspect and honorable.

It was probably because they didn't think he had anybody to talk to, because he generally didn't let anyone near enough to know if he was close to people or not.

And it didn't take any acrobatics to consider the possibility that the woman he was sleeping with might not realize that he felt close to *her*. Because he hadn't told her that he did, had he?

He'd actually gone out of his way not to say anything that could be construed as *too clingy*, because this was Matilda. And one thing that had always seemed to be true about her was that she was blown by the wind this way and that.

Who was he to try to trap her in one place?

And now she was running from him because she thought he didn't love her.

But this wasn't the time to do anything about that. Not here, in public. Certainly not on Wednesdays. So with the strange drumbeat of something like anxiety that kicked in whenever he considered that she might really have the completely wrong impression of his intentions, he went and sat down at the table with his brothers and sisters.

He figured it would be a reprieve at the very least.

"So when exactly did you and Matilda Stark get so tight?" Cat asked, before his butt even hit the chair. He scowled at her and she lifted her shoulder. "Wilder says that Rosie got them all down to that barn to help out the other day. Moving animals down from her cottage. And there was a lot of talk about how much help you were giving the project." She turned her gaze to Dallas, who made no attempt whatsoever to muzzle his laugh. "Because Tennessee is known for his deep concern about the welfare of animals. That's really been one of the foremost preoccupations of his life so far."

"He's basically a cat lady," Dallas murmured.

The Patricks couldn't join in with the same relish—yet, anyway—but they were all watching with avid interest.

Tennessee smiled blandly at his sister. "As a matter of fact, I'm thinking I might adopt one of Matilda's rescue dogs. He looks like a wolf. I hope he'll bite you."

Cat put a hand over her heart and fluttered her eyelashes. "Tennessee Lisle. Is that *levity*? Are you turning into a human being? What on earth could have made you a real boy after all this time?"

"I don't know if I'm a real boy," he drawled, "but I sure am real hungry. I think it's your turn to put the order in, Catalina. If that's not too much trouble."

She rolled her eyes, but she stood up. And Tennessee could feel Dallas's eyes on him when Cat went off to the counter. But the conversation moved on.

Mercifully.

"Think I'm going to stay a while," Finn was saying, sitting back in his chair and already looking like he fit in here, to Tennessee's mind. "I like it here, and I'm reliably informed that if I like a winter in a place this far up in the mountains, I owe it to myself to see the summer."

"The summer here is outstanding," Helena assured him.

"But if I decide to do that," Finn said, and he raised an eyebrow at his siblings. "And that's a big *if*, I'm not sleeping on your couch, Helena. So we'll have to see if there are any rentals around."

"That's the beauty of having a trailer," Raleigh drawled. "I never have to worry about outstaying my welcome."

"You literally ate everything in my refrigerator." Helena glared at him. "Twice this week alone."

"And you've made Mom cook you dinner almost every night," Finn chimed in. "Like you're twelve years old."

Raleigh, who in no way whatsoever resembled an innocent twelve-year-old boy, sat there in his chair, boneless and unbothered. With a grin. "It's all about nostalgia."

"You don't have a nostalgic bone in your body," Helena argued.

Raleigh grinned across the table at Dallas and Tennessee. "That's true. But my mother sure does." He looked back at Helena and Finn. "Maybe you two are too busy with your heads up your asses to notice, but Mom likes being here. She likes us all together. She likes the idea of this big happy family. So if she wants to cook me food? I'm going to eat it."

"What a martyr," Helena murmured, with the roll of her eyes.

But it was all good-natured, Tennessee thought. He could tell because they were all grinning at each other—a marked difference from his childhood. And very likely theirs, too.

Cat came back and dispensed the usual drinks, then announced that their weekly order was going in the oven. Then she flopped back down in her chair, and Tennessee looked around at this full set of siblings. Brothers. Sisters.

A real family.

It had been six full weeks now since their first pizza night here. They'd spent the first few meetings dancing around each other a little bit and referencing their childhoods a whole lot more—though always in a way that kept it light. Easy. None of the darkness that Tennessee was sure they could all roll out if they wanted.

And now it was like they were building memories rather than comparing notes on old ones. Tonight Helena was telling stories about customers at her coffee cart.

"Nothing beats the extremely grumpy ranchers," she said. "I'm supposed to know, from a single glare, the exact and precise order, even if there's been no verbal confirmation. All because the man raises horses."

"I think you mean Colton Dean," Tennessee said, and wondered if everyone at the table noticed the way Helena sat up just a little bit straighter. Like that name landed on her with some force. Interesting. "He's pretty ill-tempered. Always has been. His grandfather spends a lot of mornings in the diner and that's a major topic of conversation."

"Imagine," Cat said with a delighted sort of laugh, "being grumpy enough that *Tennessee* noted this."

Then they all sat around, having a grand old time casting aspersions upon his character in what was certainly a family bonding moment, so Tennessee let them have it. He sat back in his chair and thought about Matilda. Again. As usual. But specifically about how terrified she'd looked when she'd told him she loved him, and how fast she'd run out the door.

He thought about the crushing weight of the responsibility he'd always felt for his family, and how he'd let that guide everything. How it had made him *monastic*. How it had given him *control issues*. How it had made him prize a clean house over *puppies*, for God's sake.

How maybe, somewhere along the way, he'd let what he considered his duties become his personality.

So that even now, though she'd told him she loved him and he'd already known this was forever from the moment she'd kissed him, Matilda doubted him.

That didn't sit well with him at all.

The pizzas came. They laughed a whole lot, told more stories, and Tennessee was pretty sure that he could see them getting closer in real time. Exactly what their mothers had hoped. It didn't just feel right, it felt like this was *supposed* to happen. What their father had split, they were damn sure going to bring together.

When they finished eating, most of the group decided to stay. Only Cat said she needed to go home, and so Tennessee walked her out, claiming his usual early morning as an excuse.

Out on the street, Cat went to the truck Wilder insisted she drive through the winter and pulled out a box from the front seat.

"Will you give this to Mom?" she asked Tennessee. "If I take it up to the house myself I'll end up hanging out for much too long, and I have to study tonight."

Tennessee could not exactly say that he had to chase Matilda down without getting into a long conversation about how and why, could he? So all he did was nod.

But Cat didn't get into the driver's seat. She stood by the

side of the truck and studied him instead, seemingly impervious to the kick of cold wind rushing down from the mountains.

"Matilda Stark?" she asked again, quietly.

Tennessee nodded toward the truck door. "You just said you have to go home and study."

"The thing is, Tennessee," Cat said, with a very small smile that suggested she knew more than he wanted anyone to know right now, "you seem to forget that I am the person who knows all about the seemingly inappropriate love interest who actually turns out to be the love of your life. In case you forgot."

"Good night, Cat," Tennessee muttered, and turned around to walk across the road toward his house.

"I'll take that as confirmation," Cat called after him, loud enough that it followed him as he walked. "Because it wasn't the usual death scowl."

Tennessee did what both of his siblings would have done, if the positions had been reversed. He did not turn around. He simply lifted his middle finger into the air in her direction, and kept right on walking.

And found himself grinning a little bit at her delighted laughter as he went.

Rather than hike halfway up the hill when there was still snowpack on the ground, that icy crust on top, and a cold night settling in, he climbed into his truck and drove up instead. He pulled up in front of the old house that he kept shoveled much better than his own driveway, grabbed the box, and then, as always, let the grip of history pull at him as he walked.

It was a clear night. The old Victorian was lit up like a perfect little music box of a house, looking pretty and gracious in the dark. Higher up, the old lighthouse that Dallas had been working on for so long was casting its beams of light over the valley and rolling across the little town below.

Everyone had complained when Dallas got the light operational again. Many of them had complained to Tennessee. And now, when it was off of an evening because it needed maintenance, everyone complained about that, too.

He supposed that was the part of the history here that he forgot. Everything was done the way it always had been done, until someone came along and made it different. And then, eventually, folks got used to it. And then that was the *only* way that it should be done, as far as they were concerned.

Maybe tradition was nothing more than the stories people told, the way they told them, and who they told them to.

And maybe, after all this time, he needed to accept that when it came to the story he told himself about his family, his burdens, and the way he needed to live his life, he was an unreliable narrator.

Because the person he'd been *so sure* he was would never have gotten involved with Matilda Stark in the first place. He could fool himself all he wanted and claim it was her showing up with the puppy that had done it. But that didn't explain that cascade of memories it turned out he'd been hiding away inside of all these years.

Like he'd gone out into a winter's night when he was too

young to know better, and had been frozen in place ever since—until Matilda had come along and melted him.

The tread of his boots sounded loud on the porch, but he thought that was a good thing. It gave his mother some warning that he was approaching. This might have been his childhood home, but he hadn't lived here since high school. He always made sure that he acted more like a guest than a resident. He knocked, waited, and then let himself in. The established protocol.

And he wasn't surprised to find Jenny in the kitchen, sitting at the table with the local paper and a steaming mug of the herbal tea she liked to drink in the evenings.

"Cat wanted me to bring you this box," he told her. "I don't know what's in it."

"How lucky that I do," his mother replied, and smiled. "She picked up a package for me from the post office down in Marietta. Can I get you some tea?"

Tennessee did not want any tea. In point of fact, he did not see the purpose of tea. It either tasted like strangely aromatic water, though heated, or like dead leaves. Besides, there was that driving anxiety inside of him that was shaped like Matilda, and it was harder to ignore in the quiet of the house he'd grown up in.

And he didn't understand why he kept getting caught up in these family things when all he wanted to do was go to her.

But he also didn't say no to his mother.

So he went over to the kettle on the stove and prepared himself some steaming bilge water so he could sit down at the table and dutifully, resentfully, choke it down. Hopefully with something like a smile on his face, because she didn't like it when she only saw his stern face. As she might have mentioned a few million times.

His mother was looking at him with a kind of amused expression when he finally settled in across from her, the tea mug between his hands. And something on his face, anyway. He could make no promises about what.

"Alternatively," Jenny said after a moment, "you could just say no. That you don't like tea and that you'd rather not sit here and drink it."

Tennessee held her gaze. "For all you know I love tea. Maybe I've become a tea guy. Maybe I have a kitchen filled with nothing but tea these days."

Jenny sipped at hers. "Do you?"

He shook his head. "No."

"So while we're on the topic of things you like," Jenny said, *her* smile very real and not at all like the grimace he was afraid he was wearing, "I hope you're not going to tell me the story that I've been hearing around town. You know the one. That you've suddenly become passionately interested in animal rescue. Because I know that you haven't. I was there when you buried Angus."

Another direct hit.

"Is it so hard to believe that I care about animals?" Tennessee asked mildly. Or at least he tried to sound mild, anyway. "Why does everybody act like I'm some serial killer that would rather butcher them in my backyard?"

"I don't think anyone has suggested that," his mother

replied in that calm voice of hers that he remembered from childhood.

Usually in moments of grave injustice, when he had been outraged and she had been entirely unflappable. It only occurred to him now that maybe he'd gotten it from her—which was probably why he couldn't seem to use it when he was with her.

Jenny kept talking. "I don't think it's unreasonable that people might notice how odd it seems that when a person they've known forever, who has only ever been interested in exactly one thing—that being the family business—that he would suddenly turn around and have a brand-new interest out of nowhere." She took a very deliberate sip of her tea. "Of course, the new interest does happen to be connected to a very pretty woman."

Tennessee played with the mug in front of him. He thought about deflecting, but since he wasn't likely to give his mother the finger he'd tossed Cat's way, he rethought. "You know we've been having those dinners every week. The three of us and the Patricks."

"The LPL club," Jenny said with a smile. "I'm completely in favor of it. Assuming you're all getting along, that is, and not using it to air grievances and mire yourself in the past. We've all done far too much of that."

"We're actually getting along great," Tennessee told her. "To be honest, it's like we've known each other forever. It makes perfect sense that we're family. And it doesn't hurt that the more we hang out in public like that, the less people gossip about it. Or anyway, not where I can hear."

"Oh, people always gossip." Jenny laughed. "But I think you're right. I don't think anyone's required confirmation from me. That means they already know. And in this case, I have to say that I think the Cowboy Point grapevine has done us well."

Tennessee agreed with that. Let them gossip. "It looks like they might be sticking around, so I'm sure the gossip will kick into higher gear, sooner or later. If it's particularly juicy, I'll hear about it one of these mornings."

"You always do." Jenny sipped her tea again, her gaze on his. Expectant, he thought. Because since when did he sit around making small talk?

"Tonight we had our usual dinner and it was great," Tennessee said. "And at some point I looked around the table and I realized that they were all okay. Even Dallas."

"Dallas might or might not be okay," his mother said quietly. "But he's also the only one who can fix that."

"I think I got that, at last," Tennessee told her, the truth of that washing over him and settling deep inside him. "It's not up to me, anyway. Cat is happy. Far more happy with a Carey than I would have thought was genetically possible, but she is."

Jenny's smile widened. "She is indeed."

"So what I have to ask myself is why am I holding on so hard?" And somewhere in there, his voice got a little rough.

From across the table, Jenny's smile dropped. She blew out a breath, and then she reached over and put one of her hands on his.

"My sweet boy," she said, her eyes filled with emotion,

"you had no other choice. For years. I let you down."

"You are not the one who let me or anybody else down, Mom," he said fiercely.

"I got lost there for a while." When he went to argue, Jenny shook her head. "I did, and you know I did. And you stepped up. Do you think that I don't know how it is that you learned to cook so well, Tennessee? How you fed your brother and your sister when I couldn't? And made me eat when I wouldn't? How you dropped most of your extracurriculars so you could work in the store so that we didn't have to hire someone to pick up the slack? How you made yourself into a better version of your father than that man could ever have dreamed of being?"

"I don't think it was a straight line, not the way you're making it out to be," Tennessee said gruffly. Over the lump in his throat.

Jenny swallowed hard. "I can't take any of that back," she said quietly, sounding like she had a matching lump in her own throat. "And when I think about how I might have changed things, it gets hard, because look at the man you are. Look at all you've accomplished. How could I want that to change? I'm proud of the man you are. I just wish there was a way you could have come to him differently."

"I don't blame you for any of that," Tennessee said after a moment, though he did feel a bit as if the kitchen was spinning all around him. Because he remembered those days differently. Yes, he'd taught himself how to cook because someone had to feed Dallas and Cat and try to tempt Jenny to eat something, but he'd seen it as a duty. And duties were things that had to be done, so there was no bemoaning them. Just doing what had to be done.

"I know you don't blame me," his mother said softly now. "Sometimes I wish you would. Instead, you simply shouldered burdens that weren't yours and you've been walking with them ever since. What I hope is that you can put them down now. Because you deserve to live your *own* life, Tennessee."

"My life is fine the way it is," he argued, almost by reflex.

"If it was fine," his mother replied, her eyes on his, "I don't think that you'd be keeping Matilda Stark a secret. And keeping her secret very badly, I might add. It's not like people can't recognize her truck no matter where it's parked, Tennessee."

Meaning that what they'd hidden from the street hadn't been hidden from the windows of this house, and why hadn't that occurred to him?

He pulled his hand away and found himself scraping his hair back. It always got too long in the winter. He usually cut it by now, but Matilda liked it. "Yeah. Well. I'm not sure that's going anywhere."

But he didn't believe that. He didn't want to believe that.

And his mother just laughed.

Oddly, it made him feel better.

"Please don't tell me that you're going to do to that poor girl what you did to your high school girlfriend." When he looked at her in shock, Jenny shook her head. "Oh, Tennessee. Love isn't demanding a show of loyalty and then making unilateral decisions about what that loyalty should look like. Don't get me wrong. Kacey was a sweet girl. I liked her. But I never thought she was for you because she took you far too seriously. She never made you change course or even consider it. I don't think there's any danger of Matilda Stark doing the same."

"Mom," Tennessee said, and suddenly it was critically important that he say exactly the right thing in exactly the right way, or all would be lost. He could feel it like a heart attack inside of him. "Mom, the thing is—"

"The thing is, you grew up with a terrible role model of a parent who let herself get crushed trying to love someone who just didn't love her back," Jenny said instead of letting him finish. "But I've seen the way that Matilda looks at you. The way she's always looked at you. If you can't find a way to look at her the same way, then let her go. Because I'll tell you something, I don't think you ever truly loved Kacey. Because if you did, there's no way you could have shrugged her off like that."

He couldn't tell if that felt unfair or if she'd hit him square on. "I didn't shrug her off. I thought that she would be happier without me. And it turns out she is happier without me."

"She's happier without you because you didn't love her," his mother said, another direct hit delivered so calmly. "And deep down, I don't think you *want* to love someone the way they ought to be loved. Because you've seen how that can end. You've only seen unrequited love, and it was sad and upsetting for everyone involved. But what do you suppose would happen if you stopped keeping yourself safe? Would the world end?"

When he started to speak his mother only shook her head, and he fell quiet again, that heart attack only seeming to get stronger, except he doubted very much it would kill him. Surely the harder thing was *living* like this.

Jenny was looking at him with so much compassion that Tennessee couldn't meet her gaze. It was too much. He couldn't handle it. Because it was setting off another kind of rapid snowmelt inside of him. It was washing away every defense he'd used, even the ones he'd stopped thinking of as defenses at all. That was how long they'd been in place.

"What I want you to remember is that the fault wasn't mine in loving too much, Tennessee," Jenny said then. "There's no such thing. The fault was in loving someone who couldn't love me back and not leaving when I knew that wasn't something I could change." She paused, studying him. "Is Matilda making that same mistake right now?"

"No," Tennessee belted out, without even thinking about it. He heard his voice echo back at him, intense and inarguably loud. He ran his hand over his face and spoke more quietly this time. "God, no."

Jenny smiled, though she tried to hide it. A little, anyway. And maybe more than a little triumphantly, to his mind.

Then she picked up her tea again, as if nothing had happened. As if she hadn't wrecked him. "If that's true, Tennessee, then I don't know why you're still sitting at my table."

Tennessee let out a laugh that made it clear that his heart was just fine, or not actively trying to kill him, anyway. Then he pushed back from the table and stood up, leaving his tea untouched.

"Neither do I, Mom," he said gruffly. Then he went and kissed her on the forehead, making her laugh in delight, before he headed for the door.

Then, at last, he made his way to Matilda.

And it felt like he was finally going home.

Chapter Eleven

MATILDA HAD HER pack of dogs with her, and her huffy cats, and that was a good thing because the house felt lonely.

Rosie had moved out ages ago. The rescue animals weren't out back.

Tennessee wasn't here.

She had nothing but her thoughts, and that was pretty much the last place she wanted to muck about in tonight. Especially since her heart didn't seem to want to calm down. Or even beat properly.

If it was possible to make yourself sick by being vulnerable, she was pretty sure she had the influenza version of that. Her whole body ached.

When headlights tracked across the front window, indicating that someone was pulling into her driveway, that did not exactly help the situation. Or her broken-heart-based flu symptoms.

In the space between the slam of the truck door outside that got all her dogs barking and the time it took him to walk to her front door, Matilda felt as if she'd spun out somewhere. As if she was suddenly having some kind of out-of-body experience.

Or maybe she'd died and was looking down on this scene from the afterlife.

Because, deep down, she hadn't thought he would come after her.

She'd been sure he wouldn't, in fact.

Tennessee knocked the way he always did—two short raps against the wood. And even though she felt thrown, or frozen, or possibly also deceased, she stood up anyway. Like she was a puppet on a string.

And the funny thing about that was, if a string meant they stayed connected? Matilda would consider it. That was how gone she was about this man.

She waded through excited, furry bodies to open the door for him. And she was deeply grateful for those warm, furry bodies, then, because they jumped up to greet him. They wagged their tails furiously. Montgomery brought his favorite toy. Fran slobbered.

They all barked their greetings, demanding his attention, and they got to do that, for a minute. Until he was actually inside and she let out a sharp whistle, then ordered the dogs into the kitchen.

Then she closed the door behind her, locking the dogs away, and it was just the two of them.

Matilda cleared her throat. "Tennessee—"

"First of all—"

They both spoke at the same time. They both stopped at the same time, too.

He frowned at her, but it was a quizzical sort of frown.

Not a stern one, or an unfriendly one. She took that as a good thing.

Though she would take anything as a good thing right now. She knew that. But it made the flu-ish feeling fade, so there was that.

She nodded at him to go on.

"First of all," he said again, sounding very *deliberate*, "why did you tell me that you loved me and then take off running? Literally *running* and then driving away in a cloud of dust. Or what would have been dust if it hadn't snowed two days ago."

Matilda flushed, and waited, kind of hoping that this was a rant and he would keep going.

But he didn't. He just… waited.

While she'd been securing dogs in the kitchen, he'd come farther into the house. He'd taken off his coat and now he was standing there in just one of those flannels of his, his arms crossed, and all of that intense blue attention on her.

And he did not look particularly inclined to speak again.

"Well," Matilda said. She cleared her throat again. "I guess… Well, Tennessee, if you want the truth—"

"I do want the truth. I insist upon it."

She didn't like how *dark* he sounded then. Or maybe she meant *intense*. Either way, it seemed to skitter all over her skin like a shiver that couldn't quite render itself into being.

"I thought that was something you'd be better off processing alone," she said, and it was hard to say that to him. The next part was worse, but she forced it out. "In case you had some kind of adverse reaction to it."

"And what kind of adverse reaction did you imagine I would be having?"

Matilda blew out a breath. And something occurred to her then. Any way she looked at this, she was done for. There was no talking her way out of it. Either he loved her back, which was unimaginable and its own journey. Or he didn't, in which case, it didn't really matter what she said, did it? Her heart was smashed either way. The flu of vulnerability would carry her off, but not kill her because these things never *actually* killed anyone, and they would both live in this small valley forever, remembering what it was like to have sex with each other.

It was all awful, was the thing. So she might as well go for it.

There was no point wishing, later, that she'd said something when she could say it now. And she already felt too vulnerable to live through the next hour, so what was a little more baring her soul?

So she blew out another breath like that might help, settled her hands on her hips for a little bit of courage, and then met his gaze. That endlessly blue gaze. "The thing is, generally speaking, I am a person that people leave."

His frown deepened, but he otherwise didn't react. "Go on," he told her.

She could feel her pulse like it was battering her. In her wrists. Her neck. Behind her knees. "My parents left me, each in their own way. Quite honestly, every friend I thought I had in school left me too. I am odd."

And she nodded as she said that, as she let it sit there a

moment, because saying that out loud felt a lot like liberation. That helped her keep going. "I understand social cues, despite some rumors you might have heard over the years, but I don't necessarily heed them. I like what I like and what I *don't* like is pretending to like things that I will never like. There is a very short list of people whose opinions I care about. And I guess you're on it."

Still, Tennessee just stood there, watching her. Waiting.

Like he knew where she was going when she wasn't sure she did.

That wasn't true. She did know. So she might as well get to it.

"And..." Was she really going to do this? Her pulse pounded at her. *Go big or go home,* she told herself. And she was already home. So all that left was big, she guessed. "Actually, I had a crush on you. For a very long time. I thought it would go away, but it never did. And then, eventually, I decided that it wasn't really a crush. I decided that you could be in love with somebody whether they knew it or not. After all, you're not exactly a stranger. I know a thousand things about you and always have. And I like all those things."

His eyes were a shade of blue she'd never seen before. She thought maybe her voice had started cracking, but she kept going. "I like the way you take care of what's yours. I like how seriously you care about your family. You also make a perfect omelet *and* fries, and I don't think that should be overlooked."

"I hope I never overlook good fries."

Something in her fluttered at that, but she couldn't get sidelined. Not when she was finally saying these things to him. "I have never known you to turn down a person or creature in need, no matter how you huff and puff about it." Matilda could see he didn't like the phrase *huff and puff*, but she didn't take it back. "I used to measure boys against you and they would always come up short. Figuratively and literally. I just think that you're the best man I've ever met, and then, on top of all of that, I find you more breathtakingly beautiful by the year. And when you touch me, Tennessee, I kind of forget my own name."

Surely he would say something now, she thought. But instead, though his blue eyes looked even more brilliant than before, he continued to stay right where he was.

Standing still, his gaze trained on her.

Waiting. Still.

"So, in conclusion," she continued, and now she could hear her voice getting a little squeaky. More than a little nervous.

But somehow, saying *all the things* felt good. She had always thought that when people spoke the truth, like her mother, it was mostly used as a weapon to bludgeon others with. It had never occurred to her that there was a power in it. It made her feel more like *herself* to own these things. To stand behind them. To put them out in the world, even though she had no idea how they would be received.

Whatever happened next, she would have that. It might hurt, but she would have *herself*, and there was something powerful and comforting about that.

"In conclusion," she said again, with no squeaking this time, "I really am in love with you. And if I'm honest, I can't really understand why everyone else isn't too."

And when he still didn't say anything, like he was frozen solid there—a Tennessee statue in her living room, Matilda pressed her fingers into her own sides. Hard.

To remind herself that she, at least, had not turned to marble. "I'm not asking you to say or do anything—" she began.

But that was when Tennessee moved.

It was like liquid, a sudden *burst*, when all he did was take two steps across the room and then he was standing directly in front of her.

"Matilda." He shook his head. "Do I strike you as a casual man?"

He was so close now and that always messed with her equilibrium. It was his jaw—how perfectly cut it was. It was his height and the fact she knew his body so well now that she could already taste him. Her fingers itched to trace patterns all over those hard, mouthwatering muscles of his.

None of this was casual. It never had been.

"No," she said. "Not really."

"Not at all," he retorted.

He moved closer still and wrapped his hands around her upper arms to hold her a little bit closer. And if she really wanted to, she could put her hands out and put them on his body—

Matilda did want that, actually. So she did it.

And then the world tilted, because Tennessee smiled.

Despite her long-lived experience in not being chosen, which she had decided she would not let bother her when she was all of eighteen, even Matilda was perfectly capable of understanding that a man who had come here to order her to stay away from him would probably not smile down at her like that.

Like he'd finally discovered the sun and was sharing it with her.

Her own smile back was so wide it hurt.

"I knew the night you showed up with a puppy that you were going to be trouble," Tennessee told her. "I didn't want to let you in. I knew better. I knew you were a hurricane and you were going to knock the whole house down."

"Good," Matilda replied. "That was what I wanted. I was tired of waiting for you to notice me."

"Oh, I noticed you," he said, and muttered something that sounded a lot like *damn swimming hole.* She told herself she was imagining things, and anyway, he pulled her a little closer and kept talking. "I told myself it was just that I hadn't slept, that not sleeping was what made me feel so off-kilter, but then you showed up again the next night. My fate was sealed."

"I've always wanted to be fate," she murmured, her cheeks aching, and this time from that smile she couldn't seem to stop.

His thumbs were moving, slowly brushing back and forth where he gripped her. It sent a kind of humming all throughout her body.

She thought that maybe, just maybe, it was joy. The kind

of thing she associated with the pure, uncomplicated love of animals.

But this was a whole lot better.

This was Tennessee.

"I didn't mean to come over here that night, and I certainly meant to leave before anything happened, but instead you kissed me," he said.

Matilda shook her head a little as she gazed up at him. "I know. I was here."

"But what I need you to understand is that when you kissed me, that was it for me," Tennessee told her, and he didn't sound stern or dark or grumpy. He sounded… *sure*. "This might come as a surprise to you, but I'm a man of decision."

"In fact, this does not surprise me at all."

"I don't waffle around. When my mind is made up, that's how it stays." He was getting closer, and his hands were on her face, and she couldn't think of anything she wanted more. "Matilda, surely you realize that I'm not the *sneaking around under cover of night* type. I thought that you were and I was trying to let you be you."

That made her heart flip over in her chest. "Why would you do that?" she asked, feeling her eyes go soft.

"Because I've been in love with you the whole time," he told her, forthright and *certain* and he called *her* a hurricane. "I not only love you back, I want forever. And I want everything that entails. Marriage. Babies. Grandkids."

She felt that humming inside of her getting louder, growing in intensity, so much that it almost hurt—but it felt so good, so right. Matilda wouldn't have minded if it exploded.

"Tennessee…" she whispered, hardly able to believe that this was actually happening. That he was saying these things. That he'd come to find her instead of letting her leave.

That he had his hands on her. That he was talking about forever.

"But first," he said in that same marvelously *sure* voice of his, "I think maybe we should date a little bit. Just to see how we like it. Because I think we've been going at this backwards."

Matilda looked up at him and wondered if maybe her heart really had burst. If maybe this was the aftermath, except it was far more sparkly than the flu of vulnerability. Because everything felt golden and beautiful, and she could see everything she felt reflected in his gaze. Love, admiration, attraction, and joy.

It was like a miracle.

All of this impossible joy filling her up, filling him up too, filling up this house and hell, maybe the whole of the valley besides. As if maybe even Montana's great big sky wasn't big enough to hold it in.

And she had tried to be careful. Considerate. She had presented her love to him and then left him to do with it what he would.

But this man had come here and told her that not only did he love her back, but he wanted all those things that Matilda had assumed for some time would never be hers.

"I know that I'm a little off the beaten path," she told him. "I mean, as a human."

"I'll tell you right now," he said, in his sternest voice, and it licked through her in a completely different way, "that I am definitely not open to hearing anybody talk shit about my girl, Matilda." He leaned in closer. "Including you."

She thought that her smile might crack open then and split her whole face. Maybe it already had. She wasn't sure she had it in her to care, not when she finally understood what all her sister's books had been talking about all this time. Not when she could *feel* it like this. That somehow they had gone from two people to one entity tonight.

There was no going back from that.

And related to that kind of magic, she knew she didn't want to *date* this man.

"The thing about me," Matilda said, "as maybe you've observed over the past six weeks, or, you know, my previous whole entire life, is… When have I ever done anything the way I was supposed to?"

He grinned down at her and then kissed her, just enough to get them both a little breathless. "Tell me what that means," he said when he pulled away again.

"What if forever started right away?" she asked.

And then she got to watch as Tennessee's smile lit him up, as if he had his own sunlight beaming out from within. As if they both did.

"If you mean what I think you mean," he said, low and gruff and as sure as ever, "my answer is yes. A thousand times yes."

And when he kissed her the next time, she kissed him back. Then they started celebrating right then and there, because suddenly, forever was within reach.

It was everywhere.

Early the next morning, they gathered their things from her house and then his. Matilda sat on a stool in the diner and smiled blandly at the regulars when they trickled in at five on the dot.

Then, because she didn't like sitting around with nothing to do, when she was finished eating the breakfast that Tennessee made her—without asking, because he knew what she liked—she busied herself in the kitchen. Wiping up, washing dishes.

And when he closed the place early with a sign on the door saying he'd be back in the morning, they drove out of town. They headed down into Marietta and hit up the courthouse, where they applied for a marriage license and because this was Montana, got married on the spot.

They didn't exchange rings. They held hands and had to stop the truck to kiss a lot all the way back up the hill to Cowboy Point.

Then they ate at Mountain Mama Pizza that same night, on their very first public date, so that everyone could start catching up to where they'd been for a while now.

And really, Matilda thought, as she sat at a table with Tennessee's arm around her shoulders and the Bennett sisters' delicious concoctions on her plate and in her belly, this was the way to do it.

Forever was already sorted, so they had all the time in the world to figure out exactly what they wanted that to look like.

Because they already knew how it was going to end.
The two of them, together.
Everything else was purely optional.

Epilogue

J ENNY LISLE WAS remarkably pleased with herself.

Cowboy Point was welcoming in spring with a buzz of reaction to stern, unyielding, straightlaced Tennessee *actually dating* ditzy, odd, generally disheveled Matilda Stark. They were talking about it everywhere. They weren't pretending anymore.

Jenny thought it was great. For the town and the newly dating couple.

Though Jenny thought that her son, who looked deeply satisfied himself and also *at peace* for the first time that she could remember, was doing a little more than just *dating*.

She decided she would keep her peace on that, unless and until he decided to talk about it. Or turned up for tea he didn't want again, the way he'd done when he was a closed-off teenager, too. Not that she would remind him of that. He might be in love, but he was still prickly.

That was how she knew he was hers, she supposed.

In the meantime, Tennessee formally adopted a dog from Matilda's rescue. The creature looked like some kind of husky mixed with a wolf, with arctic-blue eyes and an immediate and unwavering loyalty to his new owner.

Tennessee called him Ace. And Ace sat in the diner like he was keeping watch and keeping the old men in line. Other than Tennessee, he let only Matilda pet him.

And as spring really got going in the way it only could in Montana—slowly, intermittently, every flower followed by a good snowstorm, just to keep everyone honest—Jenny was sure she wasn't the only one who noticed that Matilda spent less and less time up the hill in her cottage, and more time at Tennessee's house.

A lot like they'd both found their way home.

And when, a couple of months after that night that Tennessee had come to her house with a box and they'd cleared the air on some things that Jenny thought were half a lifetime overdue, Tennessee confessed that he and Matilda had eloped?

She'd suspected as much, but she didn't say that.

"Good," Jenny said instead, and hugged him tight. "That's what I hoped you'd do."

Then, when he brought Matilda over so they could have dinner, Jenny hugged her too, and kissed her on her cheek. And while she didn't come out and *say* that she intended to be a better mother to Matilda than her own had ever been, she hoped that it was obvious.

Especially in the way she whispered, fiercely, "We are so glad to have you in this family, Matilda. I've always wanted another daughter."

Matilda smiled back at her so wide, so bright, it almost—but not quite—concealed the tears in her eyes.

Jenny was pretty sure she could not have been happier.

"We're keeping it a secret," Tennessee told her. "Not because there's anything wrong with us eloping, because there sure as hell is not."

"Just because it's ours," Matilda said, looking at Tennessee like he hung the moon. But then, he was looking at her the same way. "Just for a while."

"Just until people get used to commenting on what you do," Jenny murmured, her eyes on her plate, where Tennessee had prepared one of his signature meals that was almost too good to be believed. "And taking bets on when you'll break up."

When she looked up, the two of them were eyeing each other ruefully.

Jenny suspected that the news of their elopement wouldn't stay a secret for long.

She and Peyton sat together a few nights later, because long night phone calls had turned into what they call their *girls' nights.* Without men, *with* wine.

"One down, and four to go," Peyton said, clicking their glasses together. "Well done, Jenny."

"Thank you," Jenny said, inclining her head. "I like to take more credit for it than I probably should."

Peyton sniffed theatrically. "You are Tennessee's mother. Who else should take credit for his excellent choices if not you?"

"My thoughts exactly," Jenny agreed.

It had been quite a week. That Tennessee and Matilda had eloped was everyone's favorite story and Jenny had been called by pretty much every person she had ever met in this community, asking if she knew the news.

She'd been delighted to let them know that of course she knew. And when the caller in question was a little too intense for her liking, she followed it up with a careful, "*Oh.* Did you not see this coming? How odd."

Because motherly duty was one thing, but a girl did like to have her fun.

And besides, if Matilda was pregnant the way certain people claimed she had to be, there was no need to gossip about it. The baby would tell its own tale when it arrived.

Or no baby would arrive, and there would be some crestfallen faces around town. Win/win, as far as Jenny was concerned.

Now she and Peyton sat in companionable silence. Sometimes they listened to music. Sometimes they watched movies. Sometimes they talked, though more and more they talked less about the past. She thought both of them liked that.

Jenny didn't want to say it, because she worried that it was perhaps getting ahead of herself, but as far as she was concerned, Peyton Patrick had become her very best friend. Patrick might have been useless, but he'd brought them all together despite his failings.

Life was a funny thing.

That night, the fire danced in the grate and the two of them sat in a cheerful sort of quiet, and Jenny had the very deep pleasure of knowing that another one of her children had escaped the curse of their father.

To say that she was feeling expansive was putting it mildly.

"Peyton," she said, leaning in. "Tell me. Have you by any chance seen the way your Finn reacts when he is anywhere near Kitty Bennett?"

Beside her on the couch, Peyton smiled.

And just like that, the game was on.

Again.

Jenny didn't want to jinx anything, but she liked their odds.

The End

If you enjoyed *The Cowboy's Least Likely Bride,*
you'll love the other books in…

Family Matters of Cowboy Point Series

Book 1: *The Cowboy's Least Likely Bride*

Book 2: *The Cowboy's Pretend Bride*

Available now at your favorite online retailer!

More Books by Megan Crane

The Careys of Cowboy Point series
Book 1: *The Cowboy's Mail-Order Bride*
Book 2: *The Cowboy's Forbidden Bride*
Book 3: *The Cowboy's Secret Babies*
Book 4: *The Cowboy's Best Friend*
Book 5: *A Christmas Baby for the Cowboy*

The Flint Brothers Take Montana series
Book 1: *Tempt Me, Cowboy*
Book 2: *Please Me, Cowboy*
Book 3: *Tempt Me Please, Cowboy*

The Greys of Montana Series
Book 1: *Come Home for Christmas, Cowboy*
Book 2: *In Bed with the Bachelor*
Book 3: *Project Virgin*
Book 4: *Most Dangerous Cowboy*
Book 5: *Have Yourself a Crazy Little Christmas*

Other titles

A Game of Brides
I Love the 80s
Once More with Feeling

Available now at your favorite online retailer!

About the Author

USA Today bestselling, multi-award-nominated, and critically-acclaimed author Megan Crane has written more than 145 books, and shows no sign of slowing down. She publishes romance as **Megan Crane** and **M.M. Crane** with an exciting backlist of women's fiction, rom-coms, chick lit, and young adult novels. She's also won a large and loyal fanbase as **Caitlin Crews** with Harlequin Presents, Harlequin Dare, Harlequin Historical, and contemporary cowboy books. And for paranormal fun, Megan partners with Nicole Helm to publish as **Hazel Beck** for her witchy rom-com novels.

Megan has a Masters and Ph.D. in English Literature, has taught creative writing classes in places like UCLA

Extension's prestigious Writers' Program, and is always available to give workshops (or her opinion). She lives in the Pacific Northwest with her comic book artist husband, though, at any given time, she is likely to either be huddled in a coffee shop somewhere or off traveling the world. Preferably both.

Thank you for reading

The Cowboy's Least Likely Bride

If you enjoyed this book, you can find more from all our great authors at TulePublishing.com, or from your favorite online retailer.

Printed in Dunstable, United Kingdom